John C. (John Codman) Hurd

The Centennial of a Revolution

An Address by a Revolutionist

John C. (John Codman) Hurd

The Centennial of a Revolution
An Address by a Revolutionist

ISBN/EAN: 9783337227401

Printed in Europe, USA, Canada, Australia, Japan

Cover: Foto ©Andreas Hilbeck / pixelio.de

More available books at **www.hansebooks.com**

THE CENTENNIAL

OF A

REVOLUTION:

AN ADDRESS

BY

A REVOLUTIONIST

———

NEW YORK & LONDON
G. P. PUTNAM'S SONS
The Knickerbocker Press
1888

THE CENTENNIAL

OF A

REVOLUTION

AN ADDRESS BY A REVOLUTIONIST.

FELLOW SUBJECTS:—

WE celebrated the 17th of September, 1887, as the centennial anniversary of an event which we chose to call the Adoption of the Constitution of the United States.

The annual return, in the calendàr of months, of a day remarked only as coincident with the date of a past event, however great its importance, should not be enough to give it the observance of an anniversary. All true anniversaries look backward upon something which, having once been, has ever since continued to be: not on anything which once was, but is now no longer. For the record of deeds done and things which have been, the inscription of their days and years in the stony mausoleums of history is sufficient. The anniversary, to be one—to be a "return of the day"—should mark another year of duration. The 22d of Febru-

I

ary, recurring, may mark for us another year of continuation for that political achievement for which Washington stands as representative of his generation's claim on memory. If that achievement has become a dead thing, the recollection of his birthday is only a ghost haunting a sepulchre, and we must choose the natal day of some hero of our more modern history for stimulating the patriotic instincts. Anniversary—annual or centennial—asserts continuance. No index by the finger of time which reminds of what only was and has ceased to be deserves the name. The Christian era and the days commemorated year after year in its rites and churches are what they are only as the life of the Founder and the passages of His earthly existence, are reflected in the lives and discipline of a continuing body of believers.

Had we thought to observe the year 1887 as the centenary of a continuing existence—a continuing event, a continuing action, a continuing something? What and where then is that which as the thing or action, called the Adoption of the Constitution, was once and has since continued to be? Is it the adoption itself? Is that the continuing event? Or was that one of those deeds which, when done, are done once, have their effect and cease being done; having no years of duration to be numbered? You may say—Well, what if that adoption was the bare deed of a day, a month, or a year, which being once done had no continuance, was not the result the real event in the *adoption*, and was not this result an existence which then began and which could continue—the continuing Government of the United States, then ordained and established by the constitution then adopted; a government framed according to that *adoption?* Do we not see it to-day, with our eyes, as our grandfathers and great-grandfathers saw it then? What better continuing thing can there be: adoption or no adoption?

So then, we see now, do we, what our predecessors saw beginning one hundred years ago, when the constitution was adopted in a convention at Philadelphia? Very well. Suppose we should talk together a little, more or less, about this hundred-year-old existence.

By celebrating anniversaries, each successive generation thinks to identify itself with those who in other days and as its predecessors,

established the actual conditions of its own
physical, social, and political existence. Yet
to each mature individual of the human race
his conception of a century of years brings
with it the consciousness of the limited span
of his own share in that existence. A generation's continuance is brief under the guaging
of a century. We accept it as inevitable that
none who to-day act and think in the consciousness of social relations will be so acting
and thinking at the close of the century lying
before us. Four generations may be computed
to have shared the duration of the century just
passed, and we recognize that none of us who
have trod the stage of life among the last, could
also have participated in the activity of the
first of these generations. And yet you of
this generation, celebrating this centennial year,
believe that you see the same Government of
the United States which the third, the second,
and the first of those preceding generations
saw.

We assume that we are living in the one
hundredth year since a government for a country called " The United States " came into
existence ; a government acting by executing,

by legislating, by judging, by president, by congress, by judiciary. But what has been or whatever could be this government, that our fathers in their generations or we in ours should cherish its anniversaries? What is any government? Not what is government in general, or governing in the abstract, as a variety of human action; but what is *a* government, that it can be said to have begun, to continue, to exist; to be called *the*, or *this* or *that* government; *your, our, anybody's* government; to be seen or felt, talk and be talked to, as being here or there, in this or any other part of the earth? Is a government, to your minds, some group of individuals, titled and salaried, as executive, legislative, judicial functionaries, fulfilling, officially, duties prescribed, while using powers *delegated* to them as agents, under some *law* resting on the continuing existence, power and will of some one else, some person or persons to whom such officials are individually and collectively subordinate, or as an administration; while these other person or persons hold all powers of political jurisdiction in absolute independence or sovereignty, with capacity to give or withhold, delegate or recall

all or any such powers by their free command, written or unwritten ?

If the Government of the United States has, all along, been such a government only—an administration to whom the written constitution has been an authorizing act or power of attorney, or a statutory enactment resting on some continuing possession of sovereignty— then the *adoption* of that constitution should have been a continuing act of will on the part of the possessor of that sovereignty; an act which, as adoption, could continue, and which, by enduring all these one hundred years has continuously sustained that government since the day it was first instituted and ordained.

· If, on the other hand, this government by successive presidents, congresses and judiciaries did one hundred years ago, through the *adoption* of the constitution, acquire any power or powers, as power abdicated by some then existing possessor, or as surrendered by such, or as transferred once for all, so far as such possessor was concerned, and passed over, so far as sovereign power can pass by any act of its possessors, to some other person—then, the *adoption* is a dead past event, and the continuing thing for our centennial anniversary is our Government, found in the persons of our President, our Congress, our Judiciary of the United States ; the only thing or personality that can have continued, so far as anything resulting from such adoption of the constitution has continued at all.

If we, in our generation, are agreed as to which of these two views of the action called " the adoption of the Constitution of the United States " is the true one, we shall show ourselves either better or worse historical critics than our fathers in the generations which have preceded us in the century now ending. From the first hour of that so-called " adoption " the dispute has waged, mild or bitter, with words or with swords—whether it was legislative action or political transfer; power of attorney or abdication. But settled or unsettled, we might have our anniversaries as well as our ancestors : celebrate the centennial in spite of that controversy, as we individually should like it best, either as antiquarians or as politicians. We are all agreed that a hundred years are a century, that it is now a hundred years since 1787, and so have our processions, jollifications, and speechifications, with as much or as little harmony as our predecessors.

But whatever it may have been that began by that adoption in 1787, have we any assurance that it has continued to the present day: any assurance that the government of the United States, then first seen, has continued, either as government under law, resting on continuing adoption, or as government holding enumerated powers through grant, cession or abdication by an earlier possessor of those powers? Does the continued succession of presidents, senators, congressmen, justices; elected, titled, salaried, like their earliest predecessors, show, for certain, an identity and continuity of that government which began in 1787–9? May there not have been a conquest? The conqueror allowing all forms of administration, according to the written constitution and local laws, to remain though deriving, thereafter, their force from that conqueror, the administrative officials being sworn to obey the terms of the written constitution as being the order of the conqueror. Such changes have often occurred in other countries.

A conquest by a foreign power should, you

would say, have a record in the international transactions of the time. But then, in the reciprocal action of the governing and the governed, some revolutions are like conquests. Our revolution of 1776 was much like a conquest. Quite so, so far as the British empire was concerned. Somebody, or somebodies, assumed the national right to carry on war against the King and parliament of England, as a foreign power ; and the issue of force made that somebody or those somebodies what they had undertaken to be by their Declaration of Independence. But there was very little change in form of local government. Colonial laws and administrations kept their course with little or no change, so far as the lives of private citizens were concerned.

But if there has been no conquest, can you be certain that there has been no revolution since the adoption of the constitution ? In any country, if we want to know where the government, in the highest sense, is to be found—that is, upon whose will the laws and administration depend for existence—we must go back to the last conquest or to the last revolution, if there is no conqueror to be reck-

oned with. So, in England, the writers on
history and public law have referred their government to the Revolution of 1688, and,
before that, to the Norman Conquest. In
France, the government from time to time for
the last century has been known by the latest
of the successive revolutions. The present
Empire of Germany, wherever the supreme
power may be, dates from the last mixture of
conquest and revolution.

Revolution, however, is not legislative
change nor any alteration, for better or worse,
in the administration of justice between man
and man, nor any change of social relations.
The century now past has witnessed a vast
multitude of changes. Changes in extent of
knowledge of nature's conditions, moral as
well as physical. Laws have changed, affecting men in many material and moral relations.

"The old order changeth, giving place to the new."

But such change is not revolution. It is
distinct from it, even when accompanied by it.
Change, to be revolution, must be change
above law ; in that, having a resemblance to a
conquest. Change by force in the possession

of that power, whatever you may call it, which is visibly exercised in every rule submitted to as *law ;* power, the visible holding of which by some particular person or persons in a state or nation can be recognized abroad, as well as at home, and which is called, for convenience, *sovereign,* whether the holders be one, or a few, or many, and which is equally absolute power, whether the possession be called democratic or monarchic. Revolutions of this sort are interruptions of something which, until then, had continued from some earlier period. If there has been a revolution of this sort here since 1787, there is no century of continuance either for the *adoption* of the constitution or for the government then brought into being, whatever it was. Our centennial recalls only a deed, and the memory of the dead.

You may well say—How is anybody to know that there has been a revolution? Or, which is nearly the same thing, you may ask— What is the nature of the change, if there has been any? A revolution, to be one, should have produced a different investiture of the ultimate political jurisdiction from that which

was recognized in recognizing the *adoption* itself. Perhaps, in order to explain this to a
stranger, it would be necessary that he should
first be shown what the investiture had been
before 1787, and why it was that George
Washington, and other persons whom we used
to think respectable, soon afterwards took the
responsibility of regarding that constitution as
law, and of acting as a government according
to its provisions. But, as we all proposed to
celebrate the very thing, we must be supposed
to have known all about this; and those who
tell you of a revolution, since that adoption, if
you hear of any, need only show you how
things now are and you will yourselves judge
of the difference.

Well, as to any revolution during the past
century, perhaps you may think that the first
to know of such revolution would be those
who had taken a solemn oath to sustain the
constitution of the country. Sure enough, if
by the term, the constitution of the country,
we understand the possession of supreme
political power above law—the political fact
upon which all laws, including the written constitution for general government, depend; and

also, if any can be found who have taken an oath to support that political fact. But who has ever taken such an oath? A few naturalized foreigners, and by implication only, when renouncing allegiance to a former sovereign; or perhaps, by a similar implication only, some voters under military supervision in "border" States or in "reconstructed" States, about twenty-five years ago. Do you think of officers of the government? No president, senator, congressman, judge of the supreme court, no national or state official ever took such an oath before 1862. An implication of some sort of allegiance may be discerned in the act of Congress of July 2, 1862, requiring an oath framed to exclude from official position all who had been in the Confederate service. But this oath, so far as it goes beyond the older form, was rejected as unconstitutional by the Supreme Court in Garland's case. An oath of allegiance, as known in other countries, is here unknown. Some say there cannot be such, here: that there is no sovereign here and no allegiance, no oath of allegiance possible. Had there been such in 1787, the civil war, such as it was, in 1861–5, would have been an impossibility. The oath to support the Constitution—the written "adopted" Constitution as law—as long as it is law—the only oath required by the Constitution itself, or which has, thus far, the sanction of the Supreme Court, is a totally different thing. Neither revolution nor conquest, necessarily interferes with such an oath. Would you expect the Justices of the Supreme Court now on the bench to say outright, if it were the fact,—The constitution we administer as law to-day derives its authority now from a political personality distinct and different from that which "adopted" it in 1787, whatever that may have been? Why should they trouble themselves to think about it more, or even as much, as Jay and his associates at the first start? Those Justices did think, more or less, and wrangle too, more or less, as we can see in the reports, about the political question. But this question—whether this government rested on an adequate political authority—was one that each Justice had to decide, for his own satisfaction, before he undertook the office at all. He was like everybody else, as to that; and, on that question, his opinion was of no

more authority after he had taken his seat on
the bench than before. But, somehow, they
got along together well enough in applying
the instrument as law. The present Justices
will tell us that they can go on settling dis-
putes, according to the Constitution *as law*,
just as well as their predecessors. They don't,
as yet, bother with the question of a revolution
since the "adoption." Practically, they may
say, as their predecessors since 1787 had said :
Where's the use? Somebody *adopts* the constitution *as law* to-day ; and that's enough for
any one who, in accepting the office of applying a law, assumes that it is derived from some
existing political authority. We shall probably not hear of any revolution from any man
speaking as judge of any court, high or low ;
even if, as private citizen, he had heard talk of
such. If judges are necessarily statesmen as
well as office-holders, they might be expected
to have some perception of the question ; but
their opinions about the matter, as matter of
fact and not of law, are only testimony, and,
as such, important according to the extent of
perceptive faculty and honesty, but no more

evidence than the opinions of others who are not officials.

Well then, as to ordinary testimony as to the occurrence of events like revolutions: let us first look over that part of the century which many of us, not very old, may call our own times—the quarter century just ended. May not anybody who could have seen a revolution in that time be asked to testify? Sometimes those who stand further off can see a big thing better than any who have been sitting under its shadow. What if we should inquire of strangers, of foreign publicists, men whose occupation is to study and record the changes of states and empires? Now we know how the English—

"Ho, ho," I think I hear you say, "hold on now; we want none of that there." Naturally enough, you will recall the attitude taken by their public men in 1861 and say that the governing classes desired the success of the secessionists, from interested motives, and that their organs of public opinion professed to regard each State at liberty, for reasons judged fit by itself, to withdraw from a union which, in view of public law, was only an international alliance. So, if anyone were to cite opinions of English writers, of whatever reputation, of that time or later, holding that the repression of the Southern Confederacy by the then administrative government and its political action, afterwards, in reconstruction, was revolutionary as regarded the preëxisting political constitution of the whole country,-- we ought to reject such testimony with contempt.

You would say—one might as well ask the opinion of Jeff Davis and the rest of the Secessionists, and of those at the North who were opposed to fighting the confederacy—those we used to call *copperheads.*

Just so. We may reasonably pretend to know better than foreigners, what our union and constitution had been; and you may say —Why should not the action of millions of compatriots who gave their means, and of thousands who gave their lives to the suppression of what they called "the rebellion" be evidence that they proposed to sustain Union and Constitution as they had before existed? Yet it would perhaps be rash to rely on this class of witnesses for a full concurrence of opinion on this point: or, to inquire very closely what the object and political expectation was, in the minds of the majority, which can be stated as corresponding with their own views of the preëxisting location of political power. It might be awkward, in celebrating the adoption of a century-old constitution as if it, or its resulting government, had continued, to take a census of opinion as to the object of the war on the part of the North; even among others of our people who, to all appearance, were distinguishable from either class of "our misguided fellow citizens,"—the rebels or their sympathizers. Would it be advisable to take an estimate of those who, agreeing or disagreeing with the Southern people in their views of the political constitution, upheld the government in the war solely on account of the anti-slavery feeling; of those who, not caring a red cent for your "*adopted*" constitution, which for years they had called " a covenant with hell," had themselves urged separation on the part of the North; who, on the same principle, were in favor of letting the " wayward sisters go in peace; " of those who recognized a right of State secession for any motive not as immoral as that of sustaining negro-slavery, and those who, as the war was protracted, made emancipation and the abrogation of all laws founded on a distinction of color the condition of their further supporting the government?

How many were there, besides, who, caring nothing for the negro question, regarded the Confederacy as having become foreign, by their States' capacity to break from the obligation of a federal compact, and who urged the war by the Northern States, as an international war to compel involuntary reunion, for the sake of their own political and material interest, regardless of any right founded on the adopted constitution? How many were there then who said, as thousands would say to-day—I may be inconsistent in supporting the government in this particular case, but, right or wrong, I would go with my own State?

If such a census of individual opinions could be taken, we might infer that, whatever "the war for the union" may have been in its result, it could not have been one in which a majority of the people of the whole country proposed to sustain our constitution of 1787.

But, leaving all such defenders of " the union as it was, and the constitution as it is " to reconcile themselves to themselves, when they join in our centennial, how many are there to-day at the end of the quarter century, promi-nent persons, who have claimed—as the result of the war—not the sustentation of that *adop-tion* but its destruction ; who tell us plainly that a change has taken place; a political change ; more than one of laws and statutes, of measures and of men, being a shifting in the possession of supreme unitary power : not merely a modified distribution of power, agreed upon between a " North " and a " South " to enlarge the powers of a general government, nor yet by a voluntary surrender of specific powers by the requisite number of States, in the way of Constitutional Amendment, but a change which was compulsory as to all the States, Northern or Southern, " loyal" or " dis-loyal"; placing all independent political power in one central hand ; to be found somewhere, where it was not before ; a hand, now, not under but above the written constitution ;

because now above the consent of any or all the States.

There are thousands, tens of thousands among us who are industriously nursing this notion, more or less distinctly ; who rejoice and glorify themselves as good patriots, and that in all sincerity, in trying to believe that this change was effected *by force*. So that, as to the question whether the constitution framed in 1787 has been superseded during the last quarter of a century by a revolution,—there is a pretty loud showing of most sweet voices, discordant enough except as to the fact that there was a revolution about twenty-five years ago, some recognizing it with scorn and hate, while still cherishing the memory of a lost cause ; some exalting it as a measure of government, extraordinary indeed, but justified simply as vindicating their own private theories of public morality ; and others, thoroughly and with full consideration, accepting it as a change bringing grander hopes to themselves, to their children and to their countrymen. Pleased or displeased, they, or you perhaps, or a majority of us, are a multitude of witnesses agreed as

to the fact ; ourselves corroborating the ver-
dict of English observers, whose record of their
times, whether we may like it or not, will be
noticed in making up the world-history.

Do you suppose that only the unreflecting
vulgar, dazzled by the military display of civil
war, and crying ha, ha ! like Job's horse, amid
the thunders of the captains and the shoutings,
are the ones to talk about a *revolution* since
1861 ?

Well, then, you may call it what you please ;
but, if the constitution adopted a century ago,
or the form of government then first organized,
has, by any means whatever, been essentially
changed, either for good or for evil, your anniversaries of adoption came to an end some time
before September 17, 1887.   It was a very ap-
posite comment, just after that date, of a very
influential critical authority, with regard to
this same question of the existence of a centennial of continuance :

" It is rather curious that amid the numerous
comments which the celebration of the Constitution has called forth, so little mention has
been made of the failure of the instrument to

overcome the main difficulties in the way of its original framers."*

After a summary statement of the discordant influences in different sections, arising mainly from different views of negro slavery, the writer remarks : —

" When these things are taken into account we think it will be generally admitted that the Constitution may fairly be considered as having existed in what may be called a provisional or experimental stage down to 1861, and that a very large share of whatever glory is due to its framers belongs of right to the men of the generation now passing away. They, twenty-five years ago, resolved that they would cure its defects at whatever cost, and put it into an undeniably permanent shape, and did so amid difficulties compared to which those of the convention of 1787 were a mere trifle."

And, farther on :—

" Consider again the condition of doubt in which the old Constitution left a large part of the population as to the real seat of sovereignty in the United States. . . . . It fell to the lot

---

*The *Nation:* Sep. 22, 1887. Editorial " Some Things Overlooked at the Centennial."

of the men of 1861 to settle once for all whether the Federal Government was a national government or not, and they settled it at a cost from which the men of 1787 would undoubtedly have shrunk in dismay. They gave the Constitution that final sanction without which no government is ever strong or ever can command general obedience—the sanction, namely, which comes from the knowledge that it has irresistible physical force at its back."

And, farther on :—

"The men who revised the Constitution in 1863–5 and who have given it to us in a shape which will probably undergo no great change as long as the social organization continues what it is at present, did not hesitate to ask the people to say whether the Federal Government had that final sanction without which no government, however deftly framed on paper, can properly be considered a government at all. They got the answer they expected and desired, but it required enormous wisdom and courage to ask the question boldly, and to turn the answer to its proper account."

And in conclusion, a very logical conclusion

from the historical statement thus given, is the
writer's remark—far more to the point than
all the splurge at Philadelphia, last September.

" In view of all this, it seems to us as if a
very large part of whatever fame the construction of the Federal Government reflects on the
American people, is due to those who gave the
organic law its final revision ; and we think it
by no means unlikely that those who celebrate
the next centennial of the Constitution will be
disposed to put the date in 1865 rather than
in 1787, or will, at all events, hesitate between
the two years."

All this is well enough, as to the point of a
continuing centenary. But it is not so strong
in describing the event as a " revision," " final "
or otherwise of the " organic law"; if by
" law" here we are to understand what we all
understand as *law*. It is a paltering statement
to say that somebody, designated as " the men
of 1861," or "the men of the generation now
passing away," " revised "—fortunately for
them, it appears, with the approval of the
critic—the written constitution of 1787, by
getting some new provisions engrossed in it,
to increase the authority of " the former (?)

Federal Government." For it is not so much that a written constitution has been revised or changed or destroyed, by written Amendments, as that the *adoption* of any constitution has changed. Our constitution, as *law*, survives or revives by resting on a new authority, as it might in the case of a conquest. It is now for us to hold that, while good enough for the present at least, as a law, the authority to which it had been referred, before 1861—whatever that may have been—had proved inadequate to the general purpose of the *good of the whole country* or *the Union*, taken in that sense. It is to be held, that with that basis for the written constitution which as " adoption "—whatever that may have been—we proposed to celebrate, last September, the maintenance of *the Union* in that sense, was impossible, and that as *this Union*, in that sense, has actually been sustained in 1861-5, some other authority for that constitution—some authority not known in the adoption of 1787—was to be found, or, rather, has been found in the fact—the political fact above law—that the persons who from 1861 to 1865 formed the administrative government

established under the *adopted* constitution of
1787, with their partisans, had—as "the men
of 1863-5," if you like—exercised and held,
independently of such constitution, all powers
necessary to the continued existence, in their
successors, of a government absolute, or without living superiors; becoming a government
as political fact above law; the constitution,
thereafter being *theirs*, or resting on *their* will
—on *their adoption.*

As a consequence, the powers held by the
Government being held as of sovereign right,
are no longer "granted" and the powers held
by the States, severally, are no longer "reserved" as of their sovereign will, but have
become *allowed, permitted,* or *as if granted to
them*, yet not absolutely; but subject to recall
at the will of a new possessor of absolute, entire sovereignty, whose only representative, so
far as it can itself be less than sovereign, is a
Central Government, which has replaced the
former Federal Government under the written
constitution.

We may gather utterance of such opinions
in abundance out of the speeches of leading
public men, especially of such as were promi-

nent in defending the measures of the Government during the Reconstruction years; and in scattered publications of various sorts, such as reviews and magazine articles, political treatises or fragmentary essays, shortly after that time. But you can hardly take up any newspaper supporting one of the two greater political parties—naturally enough that party, which for good or for evil, held the ostensible power of the Federal Government during the period when it must have taken place—without finding the assumption of such a revolution. If you do not find it also recognized by the organs of the opposite party, it is because, though its adherents at the North supported the cause of the Union, as understood by themselves, they never felt themselves committed to approval of results which were due mainly to views of the nature of government in general and political expediency held by the party then in power, rather than to any construction of the written constitutional law.

Yet if any fundamental change has been accomplished, it will remain independently of parties or of anybody's recognition. You may individually be of either party or of no

party, but, if such revolution was the fact—
what centennial was there to celebrate in
1887? Where was the continuing event that
should still be on hand after one hundred
years?

Well, this has been a century for revolutions. Even if this was a smashing of the
political constitution, that has taken place before the eyes of the present generation, why
complain as if something beyond the common
lot had befallen us? If it is the fact, why
hesitate to say so?

But we have wandered a little from the
main inquiry which we proposed, and which is
not settled by our rejection of a revolution in
1861–5. For that inquiry related to a period
of time of which the last twenty-five years is
only a quarter part. It was whether at any
time since 1787 revolution had interrupted the
continuance of that political action whose century of existence we would have celebrated
last September. To prove a revolution since
1861 would be an answer to the point. But
there were three-quarters of a century before
that date, counting from 1787. How would it
apply to our inquiry if, some time in the course

of those seventy-five years, a revolution had taken place which had already produced that very political status, that identical location of supreme power, which these various witnesses in our own generation think they saw taking place only since the beginning of the civil war? Convenient, it might be thought, for those at the North who would shun the apparent inconsistency involved in the acceptance of a revolution, through their share in that war by which they claimed to have sustained the then existing constitution. The discovery of such a revolution at some date earlier than 1861 would stop the mouths of captious English and French who call the Northerners self-stultified in talking of a Southern "rebellion." Convenient, perhaps, for that particular purpose ; but can it be so for us who proposed to glorify the centennial of an existence since 1787? Now, let us see!

Supposing that such a revolution had at some moment in those seventy-five years before 1861 already taken place. Well, if that moment was not far, not so very far from the date of what we had called the "adoption" of the constitution, we might have a centennial celebration for that revolution which would so nearly coincide with the centennial of the adoption, supposing there was such a thing, that one could hardly distinguish them apart, at this distance of time. Now, if this revolution might have occurred at any time after the century began, why not just a year or so after? why not a few months, a few weeks or days? why not the same day—one in the morning and the other in the afternoon? Why! they might have been so close in point of time as to have become so mixed up in the historical record that this important revolution was hardly, if at all, noticed at the moment, in consequence of the fuss that was made about the more visible ceremonial of what our fathers called "adoption," whatever that was, that had for seventy-five years before 1861 appeared as the thing done and the thing continuing! But now, you see, if we can get the date of the last revolution fixed for us by this computation, it saves our century of continuance of the adoption, to celebrate in the year 1887, assuming now that you are not going to believe that there has been a revolution since

1861 to interrupt the continuance of that we called the adoption of 1787.

Will you call this "trifling with the subject?" Well; we, who trifle thus, trifle in good company. Do not condemn us, for saving your anniversaries in this way, without looking at our respectability—ours, who tell you of the revolution of 1787. There are more, perhaps, among us than you may think of the literary or college fellows, as you may sarcastically call them, who can do this sort of thing and put it in print.

You think yourselves familiar with history —with the history of your own country, at least. You learned about the revolution of 1776 at home; by the fireside, from fathers, from grandfathers; perhaps from great grandfathers who could have almost seen the thing themselves; and they had not seen and you have not heard of any revolution after that. You say you have read our histories, the standard authors. There's Bancroft ;— that he does not tell you of a revolution in 1787 or thereabouts, and in his recent volumes specially devoted to the History of the Constitution, in the opening sentence says that

"when thirteen republics formed themselves
into one commonwealth, there was no revolt
against the past, but a persistent and healthy
progress." And so with all those who before
him had written on the history of the country.
Well, without wishing to cast a slur on that
venerable man and his contemporaries or their
predecessors, the fact is—that the nearer a
man lived to those times the less he may have
known about them !

But before looking about for any revolution
in 1787, coincident with "the adoption," it is
interesting to reflect, that if there was any, at
that time, it was not the first after that of
1776 ; at least not if, for this occasion, we allow
an *usurpation* to be called a revolution ; which
last term we generally reserve for changes of
which we approve, employing *usurpation* to
designate those we discountenance. With
this understanding, we must know that there
had been a revolution after the separation
from Great Britain, that is between 1776 and
1787. Those thirteen "States"—as we may,
just for once, call them, for convenience,—
which in the Declaration of 1776 were spoken of
as *unitedly* sovereign and independent, and in

3

1783, in the treaty of Paris were acknowl-
edged, by the former sovereign of thirteen colonies, as holding *in union* those powers in war
and in peace which characterize a national existence, " had usurped the powers of the nation." Because, as we must now perceive,
those thirteen colonies had not been, because
in the nature of political science they could
not have been, the actors against Great Britain
in that revolution. They vapored immensely
in calling a Congress, sending delegates, in-
structing them, declaring this and that. But
really *they* did not achieve independence or
anything else of a political nature. *They* were
no parties in the war. A mob of men, which,
for grandeur, we must call The People or a
Nation, forcibly repressing the voices of others,
citizens or subjects like themselves, who might
differ on the question of their common interests, assumed the sovereign right of war and
so constituted themselves the possessors of
national dominion in those Colonial territories.
The colony or State, or its government representing colony or State, we must understand,
had nothing to do with this so-called revolution against the crown of England. In fact,

this was neither rebellion nor revolution ; least of all was it such on the part of any pre-existing political personality whatever. We have learned from good authority,* what it was—

" It was the development of a sentiment of national unity and independence throughout the population resident within the thirteen colonies along the Atlantic coast from New Hampshire to Georgia ; then the assembly in Philadelphia of the representatives of this entire population . . . this assembly of the young Nation's representatives it was which protested first, then waged war against the royal sovereignty and government ; and finally after two years of existence declared, as the representative of the whole People and by the authority of the whole People, the independence of the *United Colonies.* What now was the relation of the individual colony to the Nation, and to the Nation's representative—the Continental Congress? The united People had, through the

---

* The *Political Science Quarterly.* A Review Devoted to the Historical, Statistical and Comparative Study of Politics, Economics and Public Law. Edited by the Faculty of Political Science of Columbia College. Article The American Commonwealth. Vol. I. pp. 18, 19. (March, 1886).

Continental Congress, asserted their sovereignty. They were organized only in that Congress. They [that is, this " People "] had not as yet made any constitution vesting powers or reserving powers or withholding powers."

Consequently, as we must now see,—

"We must, therefore, determine the powers of the Continental Congress by regarding it as the organization of the People and the successor to the British Government. In the former capacity it was sovereign constituting power. In the latter it was central government, authorized by the general principles of the devolution of powers to succeed to all of the powers exercised by the King and Parliament over and in the colonies ; *viz.*, the functions of international government ; of intercolonial government ; and the right of participation in the purely internal government of most of the colonies, through the veto power upon the acts of their legislatures, the ultimate revision of the decisions of their higher courts and the appointment of their governors and chief judicial officers. In the former capacity, it might and should have constituted a new system of governmental organs, both central and local, with such reservations of rights and distributions of powers as it judged conducive to the welfare of the whole people ; while in the latter it should have governed with all the powers of both crown and Parliament until the new system was ready."

No matter about the histories we have read in our school-boy days—

" By all the reasons of political science and the natural devolution of powers, this was the position of the Nation and its representative, the Continental Congress, on the one side and of the commonwealths and their local governmental establishments on the other ; and there were at the moment no other reasons and norms by which to measure these relations."

But most unfortunately, as it now appears, though by "the permission and advice" of this sovereign Congress,* "conventions of the people resident within the several colonies began the work of framing paper constitutions for their local governments, while the Continental Congress, busy with the waging of the

---

* P. S. Q., I. p. 20.

war to maintain the declared independence, delayed the construction of a constitution for a permanent central government which should define the relation of the Nation and its general representative to the states and the state governments. This was the fatal error. . . . So that when the plan of the new central government, drafted by the Continental Congress itself, came to be established in 1781, it presented the system of separately sovereign and independent states—sovereign and independent now as against *each other* and not as the Declaration had it, *unitedly* sovereign and independent as against *Great Britain*—and connected with each other by a league of friendship."

That is, as severally sovereign. Some of us may think that it has been only as " *unitedly* sovereign and independent " that the States have ever existed at all. But the quotation certainly gives the common idea of the so-called Confederation.

"From provinces of the British Crown, these colonial establishments had now become, in name and theory at least, sovereign and independent States. Here certainly was mutability, construction and destruction. No one can possibly claim that the relation of local to central power in our system had not undergone within less than a decade a complete trans-formation."

No indeed; not if the state of things at the beginning of the decade was such as has just been disclosed "from the stand-point of political science." Here was the "usurpation." Now for the "revolution."

"So far as the paper constitution [of the Confederation] was concerned, this system of sovereign states in league was made immuta-ble. In fact, it lasted just eight years, and was then overthrown by revolution."*

Yes, by revolution—the thing we called by the softy name—adoption of the constitution!

"The states had usurped the powers of the Nation. They had planted themselves upon ground false to philosophy, false to history, and false to physical and ethnical relations. These powers must be wrenched from them, and they forced back into their proper subor-dination. But how could it be done? The

---

* P. S. Q. I. p. 21.

existing law provided . . . . At length two far-seeing spirits divined the means of escape from the unbearable situation. These two were Bowdoin and Hamilton, and their argument was:—The states have usurped the sovereignty of the *People of the Nation* and the *People* must reassert their sovereign power. . But this was revolution—revolution against usurpation. Bowdoin boldly proclaimed it by securing from the [usurping? What the deuce had the usurpers to do in that galley?] Massachusetts legislature an instruction to the delegates sent by it to the Confederate Congress to move in that body for the summoning of a convention of the people of the whole Confederacy to revise the constitution. But these delegates were so frightened at the revolutionary character of the proposition, that they disobeyed the command of the legislature which sent and instructed them, and never presented the project at all. On the other hand, the more politic Hamilton had recourse to one subterfuge and another; until at last, chiefly through his shrewd manipulation of opportunities, the best talent of the Nation was brought together in secret convention, and persuaded to frame a constitution withdrawing from the states the greater part of the usurped powers, and to make an appeal to the people of the Nation to establish it. The people answered with sufficient unanimity 'Yea, and the Nation reasserted its sovereignty."

You see that we can give you brave words for our claiming that no revolution has taken place since the adoption of the constitution, because that "adoption" was itself a revolution which made the revolution which some people think they saw a quarter of a century ago an impossibility; the needful thing having been done seventy-five years before, which is all we need to consider to save our centennial for us.

This historical exposure of "usurpation" as the foundation of the existence of the original states, which is to be regarded as a justification for revolution in the adoption of the constitution of 1787, is not altogether new. It was referred to by Pomeroy, with his sanction, as having been stated by Dr. McIlvaine of Princeton, writing in 1861. But the statements which have just been recited are particularly noticeable as appearing shortly before the

date which we have selected for our centennial.
These too are especially worthy of our attention as being found in a Political Science Quarterly, published under the auspices of one of
our oldest Universities, established before the
beginning of the century, in the city where
the government contemplated under the constitution was inaugurated on the 30th of April,
1789, and where fifty years afterwards the
semi-centennial of that event was commemorated by an address delivered before the New
York Historical Society by John Quincy
Adams.

In that address "the old man eloquent,"
with whom perhaps this view of the adoption,
as a revolution against usurping States, originated, presented the argument in an elaborate
restatement of our history from the colonial
era, summing up his conclusion in this passage :

"And on that day of which you now com-
memorate the fiftieth anniversary, on that
30th day of April, 1789, was the mighty revolution, not only in the affairs of our own country, but in the principles of government over
civilized man accomplished. The revolution
itself was a work of thirteen years, and had

never been completed until that day. The Declaration of Independence and the Constitution of the United States are parts of one consistent whole, founded upon one and the same theory of government ; then new, not as a theory, for it had been working itself into the mind of man for many ages, and had been especially expounded in the writings of Locke, but had never been adopted by a great nation."

Mr. Adams' view is not essentially different from that given us by our College. There is some distinction, so far as the former presents the revolution as the continuous event of thirteen years and the latter indicates the alternation of a " usurpation," sandwiched between two revolutions. If the revolutionary doings of 1776 were directed against the King of England and he had got himself out of the scrape by the treaty of 1783, the tail-end of Mr. Adams' thirteen years of revolution, finished up by "the Adoption," ought to have been against somebody else.

But Adams was equally contemptuous of the State existence. In the same address he says :—

"Where then did each State get the sovereignty, freedom and independence which the articles of Confederation declare it retains? Not from the whole people of the whole union, not from the Declaration of Independence, not from the people of the State itself. It was assumed by agreement between the legislatures of the several States and their delegates in Congress, without authority from, or consultation with, the people at all."

Mrs. E. B. Browning has said,—

" ——— Every age,
Through being beheld too close, is ill-discerned
By those who have not lived past it."

This is applicable in the present inquiry. During the century just ending, intellectual progress, at least the acquisition of learning about matters and things in general, has been wonderfully enlarged and diffused. Especially has the history of the past received new illumination. We know lots of things about what had happened and even about what had not happened long before our grandfathers lived, that they never dreamed of. Why should not we know what happened and what didn't hap-

pen in their own time better than they could.
The prehistoric mounds have been opened,
dead tongues forced to speak, hieroglyphics
have been read. But these things are essentially of the old method; like accidental finds
of musty title-deeds in a worm-eaten oaken
chest. The critical school of history has come
into being and the Positive Philosophy been
applied to history, since Bancroft and the
other historians you know of, began to tell
their plain unvarnished tale. Myths can now
be explained and made to yield historic ve-
racity. Our land may be too young for buried
cities, battered inscriptions, and unknown
tongues of the past; but we may have had
our folk-lore and myths as well as people in
other lands. The fathers—four generations
ago—would swallow almost any sort of myth,
for real history. They lived in our heroic age.
They are our heroes and as such they were
just the sort to make myths for us—were those
fathers and founders. The heroes of antiquity
always did that way, leaving funny stories,
not over cleanly, some of them, about their
deeds and adventures, which passed for won-
ders, until long, long afterwards, they were

explained as *myths* by the philosophic historian, showing that the actors were really embodiments of natural laws, forces, ideas, "physical and ethnical relations," and such like. What then was the biggest myth for our fathers? Why, it was all in the word "Adoption." They believed in adoption just as the early Romans believed in the she-wolf's suckling the Latin twins by Tiber's yellow waves. Each hero had his little legend. George Washington,—there were stories about him. But the revolution he was engaged in when he drew his sword as commander under the tree in Cambridge was not, as we used to think, the first, last and only revolution he was up to in his career. The second, we now have learned, was consummated when George Guelf, of a Hanoverian family, settled in England, with the connivance of, or being specially incited thereto by J. Adams, B. Franklin, J. Jay and H. Laurens, American commissioners and friends of our George and sent by that very same Sovereign Continental Congress; and also moved thereto by himself, too, undoubtedly, when he interviewed Cornwallis at Yorktown, interfered with our affairs and in the treaties of Paris 1782 and 1783 assumed to recognize thirteen somethings, by name, New Hampshire, Massachusetts, and so on, as Free and Independent States ; and said that he, George aforesaid, as King of England, would in the future " deal with them as such." A third revolution was this of 1787—revolution by *adoption*. Mr. Schouler, another literary man, in his popular history of the United States, says—" Nothing saved America from perdition under the so-called perpetual league but a *coup de main*. Happily the revolution which superseded the old articles had the popular sanction and was bloodless." As the term *coup de main* indicates force, the strong hand, violence, we must suppose the author may have intended *coup d'etat*. Our George may, as a boy, have suffered under a disability to tell a lie. But as he was foremost in the convention and to be so in the new dynastic arrangement, we must believe he had surmounted that early difficulty in the path of political ambition. The adoption by the convention was clearly a *plébiscite*, like those engineered by the first and third Napoleon.

In older times those who did not like the

political constitution of a country and who
wished to have the supreme power in another hand than that of the actual possessor, had only one method of being satisfied.
They were obliged to effect the desired
change by revolution, in their own day and
generation. That such revolution always involved some hazard—risk of property and perhaps of life, risk of getting the ugly name of
"traitor"—was always taken into consideration beforehand. Now if similarly dissatisfied
persons can succeed in making the past over
again, by pure literature, if they can, by writing history backwards, on scientific principles,
cause the required revolution to have taken
place before they were born in time to risk a
single hair,—why, this way is cheaper by a
good deal, and, with careful handling, their
revolution may do good service for a long
time.

"The fathers and founders," as we used to
call them, Washington, Bowdoin, Hamilton,
Ben Franklin and the rest, who were sent as
delegates by those simple-minded usurpers—
those States, were, we now see, somewhat sly
fellows. They had beguiled their States into

sending them to a convention to draw up a
plan for a better instrument for general government, and behold, in following this instruction, they accomplished a revolution against
their principals. They settled the matter for
their States, if their "adoption," 17th of September, 1787,—their agreement on a plan—was
the adoption, which was the revolution. And
that it was, we have admitted by choosing the
17th of September, 1887, as marking the centennial of the great event. The so-called
ratification by the States, by conventions or
legislatures, was a formality : very proper as a
token of State submission to the inevitable or
that the revolution was "peaceable," as our
later historians of the event term it. Mr. J.
Q. Adams appears to have had a somewhat
different opinion of the point of time from
which "adoption" should be reckoned ; if not
also as to the territorial extent of the change.
In the same address, he says—

"A constitution for the people and the distribution of legislative, executive and judicial
powers was prepared. It announced itself as
the work of the people themselves, and as this
was unquestionably a power assumed by the

4

convention, not delegated to them by the people, they religiously confined it to a simple power to propose, and carefully provided that it should be no more than a proposal, until sanctioned by the confederation Congress, by the State legislatures and by the people of the several States in conventions, specially assembled by authority of their legislatures for the single purpose of examining and passing upon it."

When Adams, in the same address, refers to the two States, Rhode Island and North Carolina, which did not join in ratifying the constitution until after the government had been inaugurated on the adoption by eleven States, he represents them as not bound by such adoption and as independent of that government; if not as foreign nations. In this he surrenders the assumption which is the basis of his doctrine of State usurpation, as it is of the statement made in the *Political Science Quarterly;* which is—that there was already in existence a single political people or Nation, which had come into being in 1776, and which included the population of every one of the thirteen. To suppose that it was the revolutionary action of this People which was exhibited in the adoption of the constitution requires the conclusion that each State of the thirteen was equally bound by it ; whenever it became binding on any. Even temporary exclusion of the two States would argue that the existence of this revolutionizing People was the result and not the cause of State adoption.

Our *Quarterly* is more consistent, in assuming that the convention, as well as the Continental Congress represented in the fullest extent the power of an existing nation, which included the population of each of the thirteen ; while State adoption was engineered by the disingenuous patriotism of a few revolutionists.

To suppose that the People, to whose will *adoption* is to be ascribed, was at any time found in eleven adopting States, only ; to be increased by the people of two others only when they, either *as States*, or as independent masses of natural persons, should join in ratification, is to surrender the whole position. The only consistent position must be that, at the moment when the constitution and government began to exist by the will of the portion of the nation occupying eleven States

each and every State of the thirteen was subject to it.

In a later article connected with this subject,* our *Quarterly* says with regard to the pro-
vision·—" The ratification of the conventions
of *nine* States shall be sufficient for the estab-
lishment of this constitution between the
States so ratifying the same,"—and to the way
the convention introduced it to the then sub-
sisting Congress:—

" It was certainly a shrewd move ; and the
proposed method of action undoubtedly corresponded much more nearly to the natural conditions and relations of our political society
than did the provision of the confederate [old
confederation] constitution, applicable to the
case ; but from a strictly legal stand-point it
was a revolutionary proposition on the part of
the convention, and the reception and approval
of this proposition by the people was a revolutionary act on their part. As tersely as I can
express it, what happened was this : The natural leaders in the nation invoked a force un-

* P. S. Q. I., p. 619: Article by the same writer, on Von
Holst's *Public Law.*

known to the constitution to assert itself as
the sovereign power, and at the same time to
declare the form of organization under which
it would act and the majority sufficient to give
validity to the act, and the regularly constituted powers felt compelled to stand aside and
see this new self-constituted sovereignty oc-
cupy the ground. They [the natural leaders?]
actually put the new system into operation
while two of the States were still holding out
against its adoption, and assumed such an attitude towards these as to make them quickly
feel that further resistance would be disastrous."

Whether the actors in this revolution—"the
natural leaders"—allowed the States, as such,
or the people as a Nation, to take this view of
the situation is immaterial, when we once ad-
mit that "subterfuge" was their proper instrument. As for "the more politic Hamilton,"
his resources in this line were equal to this
emergency; for, in the *Federalist*, No. 81, he
argued, as Madison and Marshall did also in
the Virginian Convention, that a State would
not be suable by its own citizens in the Federal
Court—*being sovereign:* that difficulty which
has been the great stumbling block for the

supreme-government theory, from the day of Chisholm *vs.* Georgia to the day of Mr. Justice Miller's reference to it in his address before the Michigan Law School, June, 1887.

From the history of this revolutionary adoption, as given by its discoverers, one might doubt whether anybody at that time, unless, perhaps, the gentlemen who formed the convention and sat it out to the 17th of September, had any purpose or intention in the matter. Fifty or sixty years ago, when Kent and Story were living, the judges and commentators, when in doubt about the interpretation of the text, would hunt up the record of some of the members of the convention and argue from their sayings or doings that this or that meaning was the meaning which the framers themselves intended the wording in the Constitution should have. This method of interpretation was, even then, more or less criticised. But now-a-days we have changed all that. We do not any more concern ourselves as to what these agents of revolution meant by the constitution they drafted, because, even if we attribute the revolution to them individually, we should do it with the suspicion that they didn't themselves know what they were about.

So a professor from another college † has just told us :—

"We must also be on our guard against attaching too much importance to the way in which the framers of the constitution understood their own action and to the motives by which they explained it. This is only another way of saying that the intellect often lags behind the impulses and feelings that govern conduct, that men are not seldom influenced by motives of which they have not given themselves an account, and that a man may even become the champion of a cause the nature and bearings of which he has not clearly discerned."

This, with many similar propositions of this school of thinkers, illustrates the observation of a contemporary French writer, Paul Bourget, that democracy is antagonistic to individual responsibility and effort in political life.

---

† Professor Richard Hudson, University of Michigan, in the article, State Autonomy *vs.* State Sovereignty, in the *New Englander and Yale Review*, p. 42, Jan., 1888.

It introduces "determinism" in politics. Men individually regard no one as particularly responsible and look on all that is done as the result of fatality ; or they refer it to *ideas*.

It is perhaps rather singular that an earlier revolution which so conveniently disposes of the charge that the North, during the civil war, was engaged in a revolutionary course, should so recently have been discovered as coinciding with the first year of the century ending in 1887. Undoubtedly, many would like to accept the state of things presented to us, as resulting from revolution, without being obliged to infer that the Fathers and Founders were either disguised tricksters, or clumsy puppets moved by unseen forces. For their satisfaction we may try to settle the nature of that which we have called, as our fathers had in 1776, the Independence of the United States.

We, in our generation, are not so far removed from that date as not to know that, at that time and earlier and ever since, there have been in this country two political schools, neither one of them favored in one section more than in another, and neither peculiar to

our country: because the partisans of each have
been seen everywhere in Europe during the
same period. For convenience, and in corre-
spondence rather with their later acceptance
than with their origin, we may distinguish
them as the English and the French schools.
The first, as illustrated by all writers on English Constitutional Law, rested on history, on
the recognition of facts known by history.
The second proposed to found all knowledge
of political fact on a statement unsupported
by history and received as matter of faith,
maintained by dogmatic assertion. In France
this was illustrated by each of the two great
political parties in deadly opposition. By one,
in asserting an inborn right, in members of
certain families, to hold the supreme power.
This they called the doctrine of "legitimacy,"
or of "divine right." But it was equally illustrated by their opponents in proclaiming that
the people, or nation, without limitation of
persons, are the sole possessors of this power.
If this party did not use the terms *divine right*
and *legitimacy* for their own doctrine, it was
not because they were not equally applicable
for it as for the doctrine of the opposing

party. A recent French author remarks : " It
has been said with reason that there are the
Ultramontanes of the rights of the people and
the Jacobins of divine right. I do not see
much difference between those who invoke
the inalienable and imprescriptible right of
popular sovereignty, in support of universal
suffrage, and those who assert the inalienable
and divine right of a family or chief, in support of absolutism." *

Sir Henry Maine, in his last work† ob-
served :—

"The enthusiasts for popular government,
particularly where it reposes on a wide basis
of suffrage, are actuated by much the same
spirit as the zealots of Legitimism. They assume their principle to have a sanction ante-
cedent to fact."

Each of these dogmatic contestants equally
disregarded facts. As to the basis of their
respective doctrines, they differed only as one
had originated in the theological period and
the other in the metaphysical period of politi-

---

* Adolphe Prins, Professor in the University of Brussels,
in *La Democratie et la Regime Parlementaire.*

† " Essay on Popular Government." p. 20.

cal speculation; recognized as successive by
M. Auguste Comte, into whose third, which is
presumptively the final period, that of the
" *Positivists*," enlightened by the *positive political science*, we are now to be inducted by
philosophers who can discern usurpations and
revolutions in past centuries by their innate
appreciation of the necessity of things necessary, of physical and ethnical relations, forces,
ideas, etc., a philosophy of determinism, in
which the will of each and every individual
person comprehended in their *nation* or *people*
is passive. But what this will require of us
individually, *as subjects*, we shall always learn
from these Comtists, or *positive* philosophers.
Personal sovereignty may become obsolete;
but this political science will answer its purpose.

Our statesmen and particularly our lawyers
when acting as statesmen, and these have for
the most part, been lawyers, have never been
distinctly of either the English historical or
the French dogmatic school; and so have
appeared as of one or of the other, as seemed
convenient for the occasion. This is notably
true of Story and of Webster—the Dioscuri of

Northern Political Theory.   In some instances,
accepting what they supposed to be the historical fact—the separate sovereignty of each of
the original thirteen States, they represented
the constitution as the result of a contract between those States to maintain a federal organ
of government.   In others, in harmony with
the dogmatic metaphysical school, they ascribed it to the people or nation acting as
superior and sovereign, by divine right, as to
the States.

But, for the most part, they have not, in
these last instances, thought of placing the
Nation's birth at 1787, or, in the former, of
ascribing the existence of the States, before
that date, to usurpation at some date after
1776, and the national supremacy, after the
adoption, to the revolutionary character of that
event.   If they rested on the sovereignty of
the people, they asserted it as visible without
interruption from 1776; or, if they asserted
the original sovereignty of each of the thirteen
States, they regarded it as commencing at the
same point of time.

It has, however, been very common with the
older champions of supremacy in the Federal

Government, as founded on popular sovereignty, to combine dogma and history in some fashion like the following formula:

Whereas, I, N. N., do hold, as matter of faith and dogma, that no government can exist which may not be attributed to the known will of the people or nation, as Rousseau and the French school understand it, or as John Locke had taught it before, and yet have accepted a commission as (Mr. Justice, Senator, or other officer, N. N.) under a constitution of government which I know had the force of law only after it had been ratified in eleven States by conventions chosen by majorities of the State electors; I, as scholar, commentator, or jurist, commit myself to saying that, in this action of the several majorities of persons voting under the particular laws of the several States, I recognize only the action of the people of the whole country or the nation, as superior to each and every State ; being herein influenced, as patriotic citizen, by the apprehension that it is only by such doctrine that the right of State secession can be denied, or various public measures, which I think desirable, can be engineered.

This sort of confession of faith has been often employed, and has done very good service for more than half a century.

But any statement, as of a fact, which is possible in the nature of things, is better than a sophism, which is against the nature of logic.

What a blessed thing it would have been for old Story if he could have recognized J. Q. Adams' revolution-discovery in his own time, and anticipated its development by the later schools of political science!

Whatever the original country of the sovereign people doctrine may be, there is at least one Frenchman who denies its visibility in the history of our adopted constitution. M. E. Boutmy, the founder and director of the existing *Ecole libre des Sciences Politiques* in Paris, in a recent work, 1885, on " The Constitutional Laws of France, England, and the United States," has said of our constitution: " This is the main fact. Here, the American people is the artificial element, and, so to speak, created by a higher power. It is so far from making the Federal Constitution that it results from it. The effectual constituting power is exercised by the several States, the only power then in existence. It is these States which are met in every line of the text, laboring to take back in detail what they had granted in gross to the national element."

Such criticism is the more remarkable as coming from a country where the dogma of a sovereign people has, for the greater part of the last hundred years, at intervals, stood for the political constitution; and most Frenchmen assume that the American revolution of 1776, and the French revolutions since 1791 are equally founded on that basis. To their minds our sovereign people have been equally visible in the Continental Congress, in that of the Confederation, and in the adoption of 1787. This being the doctrine now resulting from the discovered revolution of that last date, we may listen to another French friend whose treatise *Les Etats Unis pendant la Guerre*, founded, he says, on personal observation and acquaintance with our leading men, has been well received by the French public; thus seeing ourselves in a good French mirror.

Each State, says M. Laugel, "in fact represents in the American republic only an administrative subdivision. It is just what a depart-

ment in France might be, if only the prefects
were changed into governors named by the inhabitants, the general councils into deliberat-
ing chambers for legislating on departmental
concerns. It may be truly said that, as to administration, the State is everything; that, politically, it is nothing.''

The instructors among ourselves, to whom
we have been listening, might say that this
statement corresponded at least to the republic
of their anticipations.

In the brief record since the day when thirteen English colonies first presented themselves
before the world as constituting a single national power, there are two great events, which,
as American Legitimists, we shall always be
called to reconcile with our divine right of
popular sovereignty.

The earliest of these was when—just after
this same *adoption* of September, 1787—the
plan agreed on in the convention of framers,
for governing the entire population in many
relations of common interest for every nation, was candidly submitted to each one of
thirteen political bodies then recognized by
the world as holding together—*in a voluntary*

union and not severally—all the powers ever be-
longing to any independent nation: a plan
framed for them, though without precise in-
structions from them as to its general nature,
by good men and true; selected by themselves,
separately, and afterwards presented to them,
severally, to accept or reject as members of
that pre-existing union—in and by which and
only so—each of them had had any international recognition or any capacity, as a political personality, to accept or decline any such
plan, and when, through the majority voice of
the qualified electors, represented in special
conventions chosen by such electors, in a certain number of such political bodies, capable
in union of sustaining such plan *by force*, this
plan was accepted and, for that reason, or on
that basis as authority, was put in operation as
the supreme law for all the people of the thirteen States of that pre-existing union.

This action, or fact cognizable in history as
a political event, culminated in the inaugura-
tion in the city of New York, April 30, 1789, of
the first President of the United States, which
was commemorated in that city fifty years
afterwards, when the address by Mr. Adams,

5

entitled *The Jubilee of the Constitution* was
delivered before the New York Historical
Society.

When shall such hero live again? And, if
such is around now, will our Historical Society
present him for its celebration of the second
Jubilee ?

The later event was when, in 1861–5, certain
political bodies, identical in nature with those
earlier thirteen, and remaining in their original
voluntary union, with the intention of sustaining *by force* that same plan of government,—
an intention shown by the action of majorities
of their qualified electors in continuing to
elect Presidents, Senators, and Congressmen to
constitute an organ of national government,
and in raising armies at their call, did—as
such political bodies in union, and not otherwise ; not as a mere mass of population or as
" the men of 1881–5," or as a crowd prompted
by their own private notions of right and
wrong—enable the persons so elected to maintain and continue that plan of government
over territory and population, that had been
under eleven similar political bodies which had
rejected their former participation with such

others in sustaining the position of a sovereign political entity or nation.

In each of these critical periods a government was, to all appearance, voluntarily supported by certain pre-existing *States* ; that is, *supported* in a different sense of the word from that in which it is said of the action of persons who, as subjects, support a governing person as matter of loyalty or duty. For, except as these States were there, giving the elective franchise to their respective voting citizens, neither President nor Congress would have existed, to constitute such government.

The older event our professors of Political Science explain as a revolution, by unconscious revolutionists, against themselves—those thirteen political personalities whose intelligent action in the matter had formerly been assumed by the unscientific historians.

The more recent event must now, and quite as easily, be explained as a continuation of the same revolution ; in which all those "relics of usurpation," the States—each and every so-called "State" were again the victims. There are many doubtless who would like to ascribe this, as well as the earlier event, to a popular demonstration, the self-assertion of the sovereign many, "the Uprising of a Great People" as an enthusiastic French friend has called it. In each instance they would attribute a political result to the wills of some bundle of units of human beings living in the country at these two periods, without even stating that they have knowledge of a majority or minority of such units then living and favoring either one of these two events, or how such a majority or minority could have a political right to bind the others, not included in such majority or minority.

But it is far neater work to get our revolutionary basis well established on the credit, or discredit, of a few fathers and founders three quarters of a century before the last event. Others, who have not this clear view of our early history, are obliged to ascribe to "the men of a generation now passing away," to "the men who revised the constitution in 1863-5," who gave it its "final sanction," that sort of patriotic chicanery which the *Political Science Quarterly* tells us was used by the framers in 1787. The eminent newspaper whose explanation of the later event we have listened to, does not, in terms, ascribe to "the men of 1863-5" the identical political thaumaturgy which is to excite our admiration in the case of Hamilton and his contemporaries; but, by saying that they "turned the answer of the people to its proper account," it leaves room only for a similar conclusion. For it is no more possible in the later event than it is in the earlier, to find the action or answer of the people, without finding it in the action or answer of certain of the States.

If there was any revolution when the constitution of 1787 became the law of the land, it was not the act of any aggregation of people or of a nation as such. It took place at the moment when eleven States assumed that, as matter of political fact, above all law, an administration, as provided for in that instrument which they *as States* had ratified, would by their authority, as so many States forming *in Union* a political sovereign unit, exercise the specified powers in the whole territory of the thirteen States, whether the remaining two should or should not, after reasonable time for consideration, by joining in the ratification, continue with them in the possession of the unitary sovereign power; as they had the political right to do, by being already members of that pre-existing political unit.

The reason, or theory, or explanation for this being in the historical fact that sovereign power has never, since the revolution or conquest of 1776, been held by any State, except as one of a number voluntarily united, with ability and purpose to maintain unitary sovereign power over all territory internationally recognized at the time as that of the United States.

If there was any revolution in 1861–5, it was not in the action of any aggregation of individuals distinguishable by opinions from other inhabitants, nor in that of any nation as a population known geographically; it must have been in the fact that certain (Northern) States, being voluntarily united in supporting their federal government as agent or instrument, assumed to do, as The United States, constituting a sovereign unit, what the eleven States in 1787–9, would have had the right and power as a political unit to do, and did, thereupon, in the civil war maintain the powers delegated to the federal government under their sole authority and will, at that time expressed in the constitution, over the whole territory and population of the States, including that of eleven (Southern) States that had relinquished the only right of dominion which any State had ever possessed ; that is—the political right, as members of one political unit, to sustain *in Union* a federal government while exercising local government ; which States, therefore, in accordance with such pre-existing investiture of sovereignty, were practically treated as Territorial districts and became States again by re-admission.

But in neither of these events was there any revolution. There was no forcible shifting of the possession of sovereign power : because the possession of sovereign national power by States voluntarily in union and not otherwise, nor severally, had been, as political fact above law, above science, above reason for that matter, the basis of all national existence from its beginning in the revolution of 1776.

In either event it was not *revolution* but *evolution ;* the necessary development and continuance of one pre-existent national state, in which the entirety of any nation's sovereign power was, as matter of fact known by history and not by doctrine or science, held and exercised by a union of " States," individually distinguishable by mutual recognition as voluntarily sustaining, by force, their united possession of this power over all territory which had at any time been held as included in States or Territory of that Union.

Hobbes said, some time ago, that when reason is against a man, then the man will be against reason. And it may be said as well, that when facts are against a man, then the man will be against the facts. Somebody has said that we cannot escape history. But the positive philosophy of our college friends shows us that nothing is easier.

Appearances, we know, are deceitful. In appearance, each State—that is, certain electors using their franchise to elect a representative government, a right held by each voter individually by a State law resting on the will of other such voters in the same State as a separate political person or body—had held, and, in appearance, continued to hold political power, while in a voluntary union with other similar States and never otherwise. Such

States, being in a voluntary union and never otherwise, have from first to last, appeared holding the power of an independent nation over a domain geographically distinguished as States and Territories of such union, and, for one hundred and twelve years, have in consequence of this appearance, been recognized by the rest of the world as holding that power, not severally, but only as that voluntary union.

Appearances are deceitful. Hence, skepticism is always necessary to clear the ground for a foundation for a faith of some sort. The first object of any revolutionary school must be not so much "to inspire belief" as to excite a more or less modest skepticism : even if it leads us to question some of those lectures on our political history with which the Justices of the Supreme Court have occasionally enriched their legal "opinions."

Nobody undertakes to say whether the Justices of the Supreme Court, while repeatedly describing our political system as "an indestructible union of indestructible and immutable States," supposed or did not suppose they were recognizing our legitimist doctrine of States subject to a sovereign Government, or

to a sovereign People.   But, by their profess-
ing to acknowledge the eleven members of the
so-called Confederacy as continuing States of
the United States during the Civil War and
the Reconstruction era, their political dictum
seems to tally with the theory of a sovereign
President, Congress and Judiciary, holding independent power over each and every State.
If accepted as political fact, it lays a good
foundation for the theory.   It follows that
any State may be treated in the same style—
as a Territory, practically—on the judgment
of the same sovereign Government.

Our professors of Political Science appear
to have understood the dictum of the Court as
a re-assertion of State sovereignty, rather than
of the opposite ;   and, while urging a plea for
" skepticism in politics," very logically, on
their own theories, flout this attempt to make
history by judicial decision, when the position
of States and the Government can be explained
scientifically by positive philosophy.   It really
matters not what was done in reference to
those disturbed districts.   States they were
not, after engaging in secession ;   because they
had not been States before that time.

Whether there was a State or a people of a State, one hundred years ago, to have a mind of its own—or was not—neither State nor people of a State could continue after that revolution of 1787. " There is really no such thing as the people *of* a commonwealth [State] in a sound view of our political and social system ; there is only the people of the Nation residing *within* the commonwealth. The People is a national conception and preserves its integrity against government only as a Nation." *

As now enlightened, it must seem to us also " that the great vitiating principle of the most of our political and judicial reasoning is this dogma that our political system is an indestructible union of immutable States;" that it "is an abstraction which has no warrant either in history or present fact or tendency," and " that the perpetuity of our Union [whatever that may be when there are no States to be united] depends primarily upon the existence of certain geographical relations and ethnical conditions."†

We were much annoyed, during the civil

---

war troubles, when some English advocate of the Southern secession claims spoke of "the United States" as only "a geographical expression," not indicating any real political existence. But now we can say exactly the same thing ; only with a totally opposite application.

Our folks should long ago have been done with that word, *the States*, for, "so thoroughgoing was the change which the relation between state and Nation now suffered [in the revolution by adoption, 1787] that we cannot longer properly speak of our local organizations as states, but as commonwealths, *i.e.*, local governments containing under the sovereignty of the Nation and the supremacy of the Nation's general governmental representative, a large element of self-government."*

So Pomeroy made a point of using *commonwealth*, for *State*.

But how we shall be any safer or make the world any wiser by saying "commonwealth,' we may not see, as yet, especially as the name has long been used and before the

---

* P. S. Q., I., p. 23.

adoption, by two of the oldest and proudest of the thirteen; but whether the name be jessamine or jimson-weed, the flower smells sweet or stinks, all the same. Probably, we may keep the name *United States* as designating "the Nation's general governmental representative" only, and parse it as a noun, singular, as Professor Pomeroy and others have done.

"Putting together" say our college friends, in conclusion of an argument to which no admiration of ours can do justice,† "all these principles, facts, and tendencies—physical, ethnological, historical, legal, and political—how can we any longer declare the cardinal doctrine of our system to be 'an indestructible union of indestructible and immutable States?' Are we not dealing in mere abstractions when we say so? Are we not giving way to an exaggerated Platonism in our political philosophy: attempting to substitute ideas *for* things, instead of seeking to find ideas *in* things?"

Well, of course, *we* must say—*Aye!* Our

---

† P. S. Q., I., p. 34.

instructors in Political Science evidently mean
that *we* shall.   There are probably some less
well-tutored individuals who would think that
attempts of this sort are illustrated in this
argumentation quite as much as in the proposition so contemptuously denounced.

The existence of the States must have been
another myth from our heroic age ; at least
after that " usurpation" of theirs came to an
end in the *adoption*, which was State suicide
all round.   The admission of new States afterwards has been a delusion.   Indeed that acute
Anglo-American, Mr. Moncure Conway, has
already catalogued our belief in the existence
of such monstrosities as one of our various
"Republican Superstitions."   We now, as
true legitimists, shall receive as object of
loyalty the population of an earth-surface,
without regard to any particular method of
expressing authority.   Our People of the
United States continues its political existence
by natural generative increase; just as any
multitude of human beings continues in Asia,
Africa or a Terra Incognita by having "physical and ethnical existence," for to such a
people our teachers attribute "governmental

existence," independently of any or all States, united or disunited, with the will to hold and exercise power, even unconsciously, since they have discovered that this was shown in the revolutionary *adoption* of 1787.

There is as much substituting *ideas* for things when a political scientist evolves the Nation, having innate power, out of his own consciousness, or by his going "back of the constitution into the domains of geography and ethnography, the womb of constitutions and of revolutions, to ask there for the principle of perpetuity in any political union," as there is in the social compact, or the glittering generalities of the 4th of July orator.*

Yet we are not to fancy that to sustain, in the future, our sovereign Nation theory we shall have to content ourselves with those Rousseau commonplaces about natural rights and natural equality which served for gilding and varnish in the Declaration of 1776, and which the primitive Justices of the Supreme Court—Wilson, Jay, Marshall and others—would twaddle about whenever they got

---

* P. S. Q., I., p. 13.

balled-up in their political disquisitions on the authority of the written constitution. John Quincy Adams, in his Jubilee and various 4th of July orations, found his sovereign people in a supposed contribution from all the Toms, Dicks and Harrys of their individual nature-given independence; a people made by the assumed consent of each inhabitant. That was well enough fifty years ago and for fifty years before that. It was the philosophy of the century.

But a philosophy that can discern a revolution after the lapse of a hundred years has no need of such a clumsy and antiquated contrivance. There was a revolution and the people did it. Therefore there is a Sovereign People.

Our *Quarterly* says with just discrimination :*

" Every student of political and legal science should divest himself, at the outset, of this pernicious doctrine of natural rights, according to which each individual, or the population of any section, is practically authorized to

---

* P. S. Q., I., p. 17.

determine in what his or its rights consist. Natural rights are at best but the ethical feeling as to what rights should be, and the more individual or particularistic that feeling is, the less, as a rule, is it to be trusted; while the more general it is, the more it is to be relied upon;" Good! and here comes in the Nation having a consciousness and a will— "and when it originates in the Nation's consciousness, it has the moral persuasiveness behind it which influences the Nation's *will* to transform it into rights. Until this happens however, the assertion of rights is but an ignorant boast or a disloyal threat."

Well said, indeed; and now, in the next place, how is the assumed Nation—our Nation—to manifest its consciousness and will, unless by the pre-existence of certain individuals holding what we call supreme political power over others? And how are any of us to know of such, as matter of palpable, tangible fact—the States having gone to Ballyhack?

Would you like to know? Of course you would. Well, then, did you ever hear of the *Commune?*

6

Communism we have all heai of, and of Communists, good, bad, and indifferent, from the days of the twelve Apostles to those of Owen, Fourier, Mr. Henry George, Dr. McGlynn, and such. But their plans for managing capital by common participation in labor and profit have nothing to do with *Commune* —in the sense of municipality, or city, ward, or township of the New England pattern. *Community* has rather much variety of senses; but we may use it as a temporary equivalent for the word we would have to borrow from our French examplars.

States, that is our "States," as we used to say, "commonwealths," rather, have no existence in the nature of things. They have not even boundaries, for the most part, more than surveyors' lines.

"No one knows now, by anything which nature has to show, either in geography or ethnology, when one crosses the line which separates two commonwealths from each other. The two natural elements in our system are now the Community and the Nation. The former is the point of real local self-government, the latter that of general self-government; and in the adjustments of the future these are the forces which will carry with them the determining power. The commonwealth government is now but a sort of middle instance."*

"Determining power"—consciousness and will—if these cannot be manifested by a population of individual human beings called "Nation," they may be by the Communities.

All this is genuine French doctrine, and of the latest *mode de Paris*. It is the doctrine that in 1870 cowed the respectable *bourgeois* of Paris under a gang of ruffian *citoyens* and enabled these, in the name of *La Commune*, for months to make face against the improvised government which claimed unlimited authority, as had all the governments since 1791— Republican, Monarchical, Imperial — in the name of the divine right of the French nation.

We remember how De Tocqueville, who was said to have revealed the United States to Europe by his Democracy in America, thought he had discovered in the self-governing *township* of the New England States, the real

---

* P. S. Q., I., p. 33.

unitary possessor of ultimate sovereignty ; as near the French idea of *Commune* as anything we have on hand at present.

And how are we, *nous autres Americains*, to know where *Nation* begins and *Commune* ends, or where *Commune* begins and *Nation* ends ? Why, plainly enough, by " reasons of political science and the natural devolution of powers." And if all who are the sovereign-many are not up to this sort of thing we, at least, in our *commune* have our College and scientific fellows to our hand, who will do even more than furnish plans of government and constitution, for us to adopt, " when so dispoged," but who will tell us, *ex cathedra*, what is and what shall be as easily as they have told us what has been, by a philosophy of determinism, excluding all personal choice, either of one or of millions.

A recent German writer on public law has, as we are told, said, " Ours is a period in which abstract ideas of the state and of man are beginning to exert again the sway held by them in 1789, 1830, and 1848." And the comment made on this, in a later number of this same " *Political Science Quarterly*" is :

" It is well that, at such a time, a great pub-
licist, such as Professor Schultze, should chal-
lenge our idealism and call us back to history
and present fact. He does not hesitate to de-
nounce the theory of atomistic popular sovereignty as error, and to present the state—the
political people in organization, no matter how
small a proportion of the population that
may be—as the true and actual, and only
legitimate sovereignty." *

We cannot say whether this *critique*, which
is by the same writer, is given as harmonizing
with the Sovereign Nation doctrine of the article in the first number. The sovereignty
which is not " atomistic popular sovereignty "
must, if there are no States to hold it, be held
by *communes*.

Whether that which the German calls error
be error or not, it is well illustrated by the
partisans of American legitimacy who proclaim
the sovereign-many, and, instead of giving
history for proof, advance a title by divine
right of the people, under the metaphysical
garnish of sovereignty by idea. They claim

---

* P. S. Q., I., p. 502.

to have presented *historical* "principles, facts, and tendencies" with others, all bunched together as "physical, ethnological, historical, legal and political," for basis of an induction ; but it is not any such recognition of the historical succession of instances of actual power-holding as has hitherto been taken for the basis of political knowledge by English and American publicists. The historical facts they rely on are such as the story of physical discovery records—facts in geology, climatology, anthropology, ethnology, cosmology, psychology and every other 'ology. They give such facts as steamboats, railroads, telegraphs, and telephones, as establishing the matured development of a centralized political existence, no matter where power was located when the written constitution was made law, and such means of intercommunication were wanting. It is nothing to them that State governments have existed here, or that governments such as monarchies, oligarchies, and federal republics have existed elsewhere from time immemorial. Such history is not science.

This school of scientific politics presents *ideas* as entitled to loyal submission, no matter whose ideas they may be ; but with the implication that only those who entertain certain ideas are to constitute the sovereign people or Nation. They do not say *thoughts*, that would be giving away the whole thing, by suggesting at once that there must be some *thinkers.* It might look too cheeky to assert plumply that they who so think have a monoply of thinking.

But whether ideas floating in our circumambient atmosphere, like bottomless cherubs, all head and wings, or thoughts put forth by living beings like ourselves, have been successfully at work on our political corporeity, matters little. Nor does it matter much whether it has been only since 1861, or from way back in 1787 ; nor whether the transformation be called revolutionary—as resulting from somebody's will, or by a determinism for which nobody is responsible — we are concerned with the question only as bearing directly on the inquiry whether there is *now* anything political which has had a continuing existence since 1787.

When we have come to seeing that the ideas which we are henceforth to accept as determining our political rights and duties, so far as we shall have any, were the ideas exploited by the working agents in what was called "the Adoption," and that this adoption was *Revolution*, then we begin to know that *Revolution* has been the continuing action; that *Revolution* is the thing whose duration in time and space we have to celebrate:—*Revolution*, which has had its Anniversaries and its Jubilee and a Centennial, and may yet have Centennials or Jubilees or Anniversaries.

It is well for us all, in our time, not to be ignorant of the purposes of those "fathers and founders" whose merit we must recognize if we celebrate our anniversaries with any show of exultation—merit of some kind—though perhaps Hamilton was only a patriotic charlatan, and Washington could sing falsetto when there was occasion. We may leave to another jubilee or centennial the question whether "the men of 1861–5" who, we are told, remodelled the imperfect mechanism of the men of 1787, were equally contemptuous of the people whose sovereign will they professed to execute. Perhaps there have been American statesmen who could say, with some of antiquity—*populus vult decipi, et decipiatur :* it is the few who do, and the many who are *done*.

But it concerns us and those who shall come after us much more to know the conditions of political existence under which we now live, whether established one hundred years ago, or during the civil war; or, at any time, through discovery by political science. As far as concerns this matter, the historical questions of time and ancestral virtue are of no importance ; and if any can show us our real situation and the nature of that which here answers to allegiance and what is now, for us individually, *loyalty,* he need not trouble himself or us about dates and anniversaries. "Let the dead past bury its dead." Shall we not gladly hail any such, and above all any who, like the teachers to whom we have been hearkening, have the courage of their opinions? And, here we may recall a remark by De Tocqueville : *

"It must not be forgotten that the author who wishes to be understood is obliged to push all his ideas to their utmost theoretical consequences and often to the verge of what

* De Tocqueville : " Democracy; " Introduction, p. 18.

is false or impracticable ; for, if it be necessary sometimes to depart from the rules of logic in action, such is not the case in discourse, and a man finds it almost as difficult to be inconsistent in his language as to be consistent in his conduct."

What then is now that political personality, begun in Revolution one hundred years ago, and improved in strength and stature by continuing Revolution since 1861, whose duration we could celebrate as centennial, though there was no hundredth year of a continuing *adoption* by States continuing to exist after that revolutionary birth ?

The personal creature then born and since developed by revolutionary vitality is our Sovereign Central Government—not an administrative government, or instrument under the will of an existing power-holder, but a government *per se*, a government *of* persons, or *by*, or *in* persons ; as absolute in reality and in all possible manifestation, by deeds, as any the world knows of :—persons regulating themselves, in ordinary or quiet times, more or less by a pledge, in a form of words called a " constitution," and continuing their governmental exist-

ence as in accord with that form of words; but
being, to themselves, the only reason for following that pledge and the only judge of that accord. There being no other visible persons
consciously holding political power, those who
constitute this government at any particular
moment hold all power and are accountable to
none.

If the people, as found in the political corporations called *the States*, existing in union as
one sovereignty, as political fact before any
written constitution, without dependence on
any but themselves as States *united*,—each
on all and all on each, maintaining one sovereignty as voluntarily united,—do not hold
the ultimate power of a nation among nations,
there is no *people* at all to hold it; because, in
the nature of things, no people, merely as inhabitants of a portion of earth-surface, ever
could consciously exercise such power or be
known as a nation among nations. The conception of a people or nation discernible by
the metaphysical humanitarian as existing in
a mass of human beings more or less discrimi-
nated by race, language or sympathies from
other masses, and located between these or

those lines of physical topography, like rivers, seas or mountains, which would be convenient as political frontiers, may have aided with other motives in stimulating revolutionary action ; but, as a basis for political recognition, it is a fancy generated from the European contests of the present century.

Our professors of Political Science have told us that the commonwealth government is now but " a sort of middle instance." To know what that means we shall probably have to apply to the professor of Logic. Our *Quarterly* adds—

" Too large for local government, too small for general, it is beginning to be regarded as a meddlesome intruder in both spheres—the tool of the strongest interest, the oppressor of the individual. This has been its history in other lands and other times ; and the mere fact that it professes to be popular here, while it has been princely or aristocratic elsewhere, will not save it from the same fate."*

It was John Austin, whose keen insight showed him, long ago, that, as the several

---

* P. S. Q., I., p. 34.

States as corporate bodies, *being united*, as political fact above law, had always exercised every jot of political power there was to exercise—they, so constituting a unit, were like an oligarchy in respect to the people or nation as a mass of individuals. If the discovery is proclaimed—that the continued existence of such a unity of such States is hostile to the liberties of the individual, the proof must rest on the idea that such a unity is identical with an oligarchy composed of single natural persons, princes or nobles; or else on the idea that every possession of sovereign power is incompatible with individual liberty, which last notion, indeed, is identical with that which is axiomatic in our *Quarterly*—the assumed sovereign people or nation—or the assumption that there can be no possession of sovereignty other than one which is imaginary. An axiomatic proposition well suited to a continuous revolution.

Can it ever be the case with us that some one hereafter will say, as De Tocqueville of his own country—"I perceive that we (in France) have destroyed those individual powers which were able single-handed to cope with

tyranny, but it is the government that has inherited the privileges of which families, corporations and individuals have been deprived ;
to the power of a small number of persons,
which if it was sometimes oppressive was often
conservative, has succeeded the weakness of
the whole community."

If a number of these States, or *commonwealths*—if anybody likes that better—being,
as matter of fact, in a voluntary political union
independently of any written provision for a
General or Federal Government, as administration, have not, at each point of time, held all
sovereignty as a nation, whether displayed in
Federal or State Government, there has been
no people or nation at all to " preserve its integrity against government," because, except
as one of a definite number of persons holding
the elective franchise by the will of the corporate State, no living man has consciously
held recognized power as against any government whatever. We may perhaps assume
that power against government such as has
been claimed by the outlaw, the brigand, the
communard, the *petroleuse*, the Anarchist, to
say nothing of the late Mr. John Brown, of

Ossawottamie, or "his soul," is not the sort which our ancient, respectable, and very well endowed college would, at present, recommend as that by which the People or Nation shall manifest its existence.

This is as true now as it was one hundred years ago, when if there was revolution on the part of anybody, the people, by the showing of these teachers, had nothing as a nation to do, consciously, in bringing it about, and the government then instituted derives no authority from them and is as little responsible to them as the Russian Czar is to the nation of Russians.

Is it nothing for us to know, no matter how, if we do but know it, that the government that appeared to our fathers as an administration, acting for a known and visible superior, recognized by the world as United *States*, has really been in possession of all sovereign political jurisdiction from its first revolutionary seizing the reins of power, whenever it was, and that it is now our self-sufficing master and ruler?

But the constitution!—you say. But the Supreme Court!—you say. The constitution? As what? As law? For whom is it law?

For this government? for certain actual persons, being the President, the Congress, the
Judiciary, for the time being? Is the Constitution law for them, they being the sovereign?
Sovereign because there is no visible, tangible
person in existence—the *States* being gone to
the dogs—to make it law, except as that government exists. It is not a law *on* or *for* them,
but a law *by* them. What is it more than a
pledge, *octroyée* by that government, by which
it proposes to continue its own existence,
being itself the only judge of its fulfilment of
that pledge?

And this Constitution of ours: is it really so
generated out of the nature of things as to be
very nearly supernatural? Did it cause its
own existence? self-created? self-sustained?
Has not a German, Professor von Holst, " in
that invaluable work upon our constitutional
history," which starts out with our French
dogma — legitimacy of a sovereign-people —
"devoted an entire chapter to what he terms
'the canonizing of the constitution,' *i.e.*, the
making of a political bible out of it : all doubts
as to the absolute truth and perfection of
which " are regarded as heresy? " The irony

of the learned Professor is certainly merited. During the first decades of this century, the never changing aspect of the Nation's leaders, mutely prostrate in credulous worship before the great fetish of our Political System, is, to say the least, touching."*

So say our Professors. Webster! Daniel! Giant shade! forgive them!

This constitution-business was another of those myths that our fathers so delighted in—like the Adoption myth. Now, when the adoption by thirteen States is an exploded fiction, why should the nominal object of adoption be any longer venerated? What is there now of sacredness in its oracles? Unless it be left in the few words of the Preamble—"We the People"—so long triumphantly proclaimed as the all-sufficient testimony to that origin which our scientists have now shown the adoption to have been—revolution and nature of things, now one hundred years continuing—always represented by a government originally called "federal" by worshippers of the great constitution-fetish?

---

* P. S. Q., I., p. 8.

And the Supreme Court?—"In all the excitements of bitter contests, involving great financial interests, power, position, and even political existence, in fact everything which could properly be brought within its judicial cognizance, the people have always felt that their interests were safely entrusted to its charge."* So says Mr. Justice Miller, in his address to the Law-graduates of Michigan University, and we will all say with him in his concluding sentence—"That the court may long continue to deserve this confidence, as it has for the past hundred years, must be the desire of every patriotic citizen."

The claim for the Court, to have faithfully, as tribunal, upheld the application of the constitution as law for those subject to law, may be proudly sustained. But what will be its position as umpire when it is itself identified with a body of persons holding the only power in the land which can be called sovereign, because not held by delegation from a personal superior, and themselves the only power-holders to make the Constitution law for any-

* P. S. Q., pp. 9, 35.

body? A court adjudicating between parties before it, in cases under known law, and a body whose opinions can determine future relations between distinct political-power-holders, being itself identified with one of them, are two very different tribunals.

In ranking *political existence* with "everything which could properly be brought within its judicial cognizance," the honored judge probably had in mind those cases, during the civil war and after, in which the court affirmed the sonorous apothegm—"an indestructible union of indestructible States," which our College *Quarterly* treats as fantastic idealism.

Political existence, in any true sense of the words, is a matter of fact; not a relation under law or determinable by courts of law. From those famous cases, in which we were puzzling Europe by insisting on the treason of the citizen while affirming the belligerent sovereignty of his State, Americans may have concluded they have solved the problem in politics which Rousseau compared with the quadrature of the circle in geometry—to find a form of government which shall place *law* above *man*. If our judiciary thought the written constitution adequate for this solution, it may be an illustration of Diderot's remark—"*Les plus mauvais politiques sont communement les jurisconsultes, parce qu'ils sont toujours tentés de rapporter les affaires publiques à la routine des affaires privées.*"

Fact—basal political fact—fact of existing power and will to *make* law—was and is and always will be the thing wanted; and this fact is now, for us, in our day, revealed. Adoption, federal compact, social compact, and every other fiction and fantasy shall be swept off to the limbo of busted superstitions. The fact is made known by Political Science—the fact of Revolution—a people continuing in a Revolution.

Our anniversaries being thus secured to us, as marking the continued duration of something the nature of which we are just beginning to understand, how shall we Americans worthily celebrate a centennial?

Will any say that all we had, personally, to do was to score one hundred and go on our way rejoicing? To smile over it if we liked it, or ignore it if we did not? But though we all have wished to celebrate this first centennial, if not for the credit of our forefathers, at least for our own self-complacency, why should we not also, even yet, celebrate it in the hope that, by so doing, those who are destined to follow us may be more secure of like anniversaries and like centennials? Was it enough to have made the Bird of Freedom scream and fly aloft in our old vain-glorious style? Can we not now, in the year between 1887 and 1889, do better by doing what those forefathers may be supposed to have been doing in the year between 1787 and 1789; by forcing ourselves to look at the consequences which should logically have followed and may yet follow that revolutionary change which they and we called "adoption"; confessing how far we may yet be from their full fruition and then pledging ourselves to promote it? Our college authorities explain that their object is not at this time "to inspire belief, but to excite scepticism." Scepticism in what? In our American jingoism, *chauvinism*—our spread-eagle-ism? No; perhaps not so much in that. *That* they may as well let us keep for use in the later progress of the Revolution. But scepticism as to our own intelligence, in not advancing more steadfastly in the same glorious path.

Now really, are not one hundred and odd years long enough, even in a nation's life, to be going about under an *alias*? Where is the sense in anybody's saying " United States " when there are no " States " to be united : no voluntary union between the simulacra that have been so miscalled? Even if there is nothing to which the name, as a noun plural, is suited, it is stupid to give the name to a Central Government, as many of our Legitimists like to do, by way of gentle insinuation that the sovereign known among nations by that name is found in the President, Congress and Judiciary for the time being. These names—States, Federal States, United States, are shadows ; silly ghosts haunting the decayed abodes of the usurpers of 1781, which now beguile and betray credulous souls.

But, as names after all, are not things, these may pass some time longer ; if not for convenience, yet for old acquaintance' sake. There are other things, more essential, as lingering assertions of the old usurped power, which should not be left to puzzle and misdirect successive generations as they have those of the last century in the matter of loyalty and allegiance. Why should the *personnel*, the embodiment of the only real holder of sovereign independent power, if any such embodiment is supposable in a Revolutionary era, depend for its very existence on the caprice of certain folk selected and qualified, individually, as electors, by themselves corporately—as being "commonwealth," or self-constituted State? How confusing to minds of even average intelligence is this bizarre arrangement; that an actually sovereign Government, the only possible representative of the only possible sovereignty, should derive its very existence from the continued good-will and diligence of some, as in 1861–7, if not of all, of a lot of subject corporations. Think " of the immense change " made in " the relation between the State and the Nation in the new system " inaugurated by the revolutionary adoption of 1787, according to our *Quarterly*, which appears to accept the common notion that, as historical fact, each State of the thirteen could, before that, claim several independence as a sovereign nation.

"In the first place · *sovereignty* could no longer be claimed as a state attribute, nor *separate* independence. Sovereignty resided alone in the *people* of the whole Nation and a state could be legally bound in organic changes against its will. In the second place, it withdrew all of the really political functions from the states and vested them in the Nation's governmental representative : *viz.*,—the powers of war and peace, of diplomacy and commerce, the regulation of internal intercourse, of finance and the monetary system, of the military system and of the local governmental system [that is, of what we used to call the *State* government]. It left to the states thus mainly jural and police functions."*

How absurd then that such an apparently "real political function" as determining the continued existence of the very government now vested with all the *really* "real political functions" should remain with these shadows of states, these commonwealths.

This silly discrepancy in the work of the revolutionist fathers of 1787 is, with two

* P. S. Q., I., p. 22

others, like the constant affirmation in a
monarchical country of the claims of a fallen
dynasty; yet—"For seventy-two years, only
the span of a single human life, we lived under
this relation of commonwealths to Nation.
For seventy years we imagined it permanent and perfect, when suddenly the iron
logic of events demonstrated the fact that still
too much had been left under the control of
the local organizations, and that the Nation
must narrow still further their sphere of
action."*

Something was effected in 1865–7, in the
direction of nationalizing the whole of our
private law, by limiting the powers of all these
"local organizations," North and South, by
constitutional Amendments. This seemed to
be of some importance, even then. But some
time or other we shall find that—

" Here was another immense change in the
relation of commonwealth to Nation. . . .
By this last change the commonwealths have
been substantially assigned to the office of
administering the system of private law be-

---

* P. S. Q., I., p. 23.

tween persons resident within their bounds
and supplementing its defects, and exercising
the police power in behalf of the community
[*commune?*] against the too wide extension of
individual rights—all upon the basis, however,
of fundamental principles prescribed by the
Nation, and upheld by the Nation's organs of
central government. In the way, however, of
their complete relegation to this position stand
three things. The first is their large control,
legislative and administrative, over the elections of the organs of the central government.
The second is the election of the members of
the national senate by the commonwealth legislatures. And the third is the equal representation of the commonwealths in the national senate. The first may be changed, except as to the election of the electors of the
national executive, by a simple law passed by
the national legislature. The second, and that
part of the first not subject to the legislation
of Congress [qualification of voters, perhaps?],
may be changed by the general process of
amendment prescribed in the constitution.
But the third is the stronghold of confederat-
ism, and most probably cannot be changed

save by a revolutionary act. They are all relics of the usurpation of 1781."*

We used to think the late Professor Pomeroy a pretty stiff legitimist for his day. But with all his talk about the Nation as the sole authority for any constitution, and his qualified acceptance of the discovery of revolution in 1787 against State usurpation, he, rather inconsistently perhaps, still fancied the States as having powers to give or withhold. He had not enough *sand*, quite, for the continuing Revolution. He said,—

"It is certainly however, an anomaly, that the general government of the United States should have no control over its own delegates in Congress; that it should be powerless to define the qualifications of congressional electors. It must be conceded that this is a defect in our organic law which needs amendment. It was a necessary and unfortunate concession to the theory of State sovereignty and independence. One code of rules should certainly prevail throughout the country to regulate the choice of representatives, and this

---

* P. S. Q., I., pp. 23-24.

should be the work of Congress or of the people in its sovereign capacity. The nation should dictate in the selection of its own legislators. The integrity of the States is sufficiently guarded by allowing to each an equal voice in the Senate, and by permitting them to appoint Senators and to control the selection of Presidential electors. The more national branch of Congress, that which comes directly from the people, should be entirely under the management of the one body politic which is represented in the general government."

Pomeroy was only giving his own idea of political expediency. He did not pretend to declare the political right or power as our *Quarterly* does. But how could he, poor man! while still dreaming of "the integrity of the States?" What an ancient fossil he was, to be sure!

That the Senate of the United States is composed of two Senators from each State— is a "relic of usurpation" as suggesting the existence of a confederacy of equals. But it is the method of electing Senators, that is, by the State legislatures, that more essentially

deserves the opprobrious designation. For
nobody has yet discovered a constitutional
clause authorizing the Central Government to
secure its own duration, so far as the Senate
is concerned, by interfering in the electoral
action of the State *legislatures.* Senators
might still be said to represent the State or
" commonwealth," as such, when chosen directly by the voting people. But, in the
golden future, when the electoral action of
that people is regulated, as well as the possession of the electoral franchise, by the central
legislature—then, when the State *legislatures*
have been compelled to surrender their
usurped power, the Central Government may
feel itself a continuing personality, like any
other sovereign.

It is the independence of the State in choosing senators; not the fact that in the Senate
the States are equally represented; that is
incongruous with the claims of a superior central existence. If there is any necessity or
advantage in having two houses for the business of a central legislature, or national parliament, there are a dozen ways for producing
either one, without distinguishing it as being

a relic of usurpation and popular blindness more than the other.

This position of a Government, in respect to its ability to provide for its own existence, —if it be a sovereign government as distinct from the agent or instrument of some external possessor of sovereignty—is such a strange anomaly that those in France who there would advocate some representative system, are probably unable to conceive of its existence. There, where there is nothing to correspond to our "relics of usurpation"—*States* as we used to think of them — and where there are only the *Départements*, the Government for the time being takes care of itself, by taking charge of the so-called Constitution.

Why should not our Central, or Imperial Government, as some like to call it, secure its own continuance by providing for, regulating and, if need be, compelling the action of voters in electing the persons to constitute its successors in its various branches and at the same time require their assent, as State, to an Amendment sanctioning this? Indeed, was not this done, virtually, in the case of some eleven "commonwealths" which, if we are not ready to throw overboard the political opinions of the Supreme Court, as unscientific, were States, at the time, as much as the others ; that is, if there are or were then any such " relics " hereabouts?

Will any say—But these were of the wicked? Somebody had to decide on that. Somebody will have to decide on the nature and degree of wickedness. If the Central Government was sovereign in that instance and accountable to none, why not equally in respect to any State? Did not the Supreme Court, during the Reconstruction era, repeatedly say that there was a " political department " of the Government, having the power to decide on such a question?

Again, such being the source and foundation of all power, civil or military, executive, legislative, and judicial, how can government here rest squarely on its true basis—a uniform folk or population—if a group of five or six puny " commonwealths " still calling themselves *States*, send the force of ten or twelve members to the Senate, when there are a dozen others, each with a present or prospec tive population larger than this entire bunch of States, sending only two apiece?

Funny? to be sure; but there's a constitutional pledge on that point, given to each State! Quotha? well, yes; to *States* and that was put in by those framers only because common folks, when summoned to ratify the constitution in 1787–8, didn't see the Revolution in it and very likely supposed that there were *States* then, and that *States* there would be, thereafter. But where is the pledge for commonwealths? Our Professors indicate that, if unreasonable, in not conforming themselves to the philosophical and physical and ethnical basis of the Nation, any such petty corporations will insist on the consideration accorded in the usurpation time to the States whose position they claim to have inherited, some more *revolution* will be *in order,* speaking rather mixedly; that is, not a whole revolution, perhaps, but a little more of the same sort, to be called *adoption* perhaps, or perhaps, a *reconstruction.* But as the loudest in maintaining the sovereign Nation doctrine have been found within their boundaries, at least since the time of Mr. Adams' Jubilee oration, it may be expected that this little group of commonwealths would exultingly unite in conforming themselves to our Legitimist doctrine, by renouncing some portion of their oligarchical prerogative.

These suggestions do not call our attention to mere legalized abuses, ignored immoralities, permissive ignorances, or to injustices like civil or social disqualifications, or monopolies, or favoritisms for some spheres of activity to the disadvantage or destruction of others. If such can be, where all are called free and equal, since all human government is imperfect, yet reformation in the line of the pursuit of happiness may be expected from a supreme legislative in new ways ; as well as by distribution of surplus-revenue in quarters where it may do most good. The anomalies we have been talking about are dislocations, congenital malformations, structural faults in the body-politic, requiring heroic treatment to save life.

It would be strange however, if, incidental to these, there were not grave disorders, wasteful of energy and preventing the free action of the vital forces of the republic.

What a waste of time and money, to say

8

nothing of nerves and brains, in what we call
the law. Why must there be a complete system of private law—law regulating relations of
persons in private life, as distinct from the
public or constitutional law—in each State or
commonwealth, big or little? Why must
each have its loads of statute-books and of
volumes of reported decisions, which have no
authority beyond the State limits? The common-law of England was said, with some
truth, a century ago, to be a general law
among the States; yet only so far as not af-
fected by State legislation, State customs and
State judge-made law. How much community
of old English common-law remains now in
State jurisprudence? Just now there is a call
for codes to displace all " common " law.
That means a code-civil and code-criminal for
each State; each one costing thousands to the
State in its production; benefiting lawyers by
the thousand. Are human conditions so different in different States? Think of the six
New England States, homogeneous in feeling
and interests, with six separate jurisprudence-
apparatus. The French *code-civil* superseded
the various laws of the provinces of old France

and, in Napoleon's time, was carried into adjoining countries, German and Italian, differing in race and language, and there remains. Think of the domestic relations, of the various laws of inheritance. Where would the Mormon question be to-day if there had been a national law of marriage and divorce? Who gets the best out of all this but the constantly increasing tribe of pettifoggers?

What is citizenship but rights under law? One citizenship—one law. Was there any *one-citizenship* under the phrase—(Article IV. of the constitution of 1787)—"The citizens of each State shall be entitled to the privileges and immunities of citizens in the several States;" that is—such as they might be by the law of the several States? Local jurisprudence was restricted at that time, more or less, by some other provisions in that constitution. Is there any more *one* law for citizenship now? Is there any more national citizenship now? Now, when after seventy-two years of weak self-complacency, always holding up the blessings of local self-government to the envious gaze of the effete monarchies, "the iron logic of events," that we have just heard about, demonstrated the Nation's obligation to clip the political wings and talons of the local organizations ? Did the Nation do more, by affecting their sphere of action in private law, when, by Article XIV. of Amendments :—

" It now placed bounds to their wide-reaching powers in the domain of the jural and police regulations, by making citizenship national, decreeing the equality of civil rights, and limiting the whole of their authority by the principle of the due process of law as interpreted by the national judiciary. Here was another immense change in the relation of commonwealth to Nation."*

What a sad thought—that the Supreme Court was not up to this "immense change " when the appeal was made to it by those revolutionist brethren who were hanged, as Anarchists, under Illinois State-citizenship law, last autumn !

Perhaps the Court might have taken a different view of such an appeal, some ten or fifteen

---

* P. S. Q., I., p. 23.

years before; for we shall be called to notice
that—

"For ten years now (1886) we have been
passing through a period of reaction against
the pronounced nationalism of the previous fifteen."*

Though perhaps it was the National legislature that should have first set to work, if—

"There is now really nothing further necessary, in the domain of constitutional law, to
enable the Nation's governmental organs to
nationalize, in fundamental principle, the
whole of our *private* law, just as there is nothing further necessary than the existing provision imposing upon these organs the duty of
maintaining republicanism in our local forms,
to enable them to nationalize at almost every
point, the whole of our *public* law."†

In a later article in the same *Quarterly*, particularly directed to this aspect of our legal
future, and contributed by another member of
the same Faculty, we are told—

"Whether it be by change of constitutional
interpretation or by direct constitutional

---

* P. S. Q., I., p. 25.   † P. S. Q. I., p. 23.

amendment, there is no doubt, I think, that the
Nation will find a way to make its law national.
No theory of State rights, no jealousy or fear
of centralization, will prevent so practical a
people as ours from satisfying its real needs." *

But how or why distinguish between public
and private law in any relation between the
Nation and the commonwealths? Does private law become public by being engrossed in
a State constitution? What are State constitutions now-a-days but imperfect codes ; by
removing so many specified relations of private persons from the ordinary power of the
State legislatures?

"The legislatures in nearly all of these recent instruments have been deprived of their
previously almost unlimited powers of legislation upon most important subjects, such as
the raising and appropriating of money, the
exercise of the right of eminent domain and
the creation of corporations?" †

Instancing these, our *Quarterly* says ‡—

---

* P. S. Q., III., p. 164.   Article, State Statute and Common Law.

† P. S. Q., I., p. 28.

‡ P. S. Q., I., p. 30.

" To these must then be added scores of provisions prohibiting absolutely legislative action
in regard to certain subjects, requiring it absolutely in regard to others, fettering special
legislation and making wide-reaching excep-
tions from its scope of action."

Then as to the State Governor. He too is
shown up as having fallen off " in dignity, importance and power," if at a more intermittent
rate. But this difference indicates something.
We may say—

" That he has lost far less than the legislature during the last forty years : which is one
more evidence of the fact that the true sphere
of the commonwealth government is administration rather than legislation. Nevertheless,
he is not regarded either by the Nation or by
the part of it resident within the particular
commonwealth, as the important personage
that he was before 1861."*

By the part of the Nation, that is, we must
suppose, by the whole population of the State,
whether voters or not, but holding political
power as a piece of sovereign nation. For, as

---

* P. S. Q., I., p. 31.

for the fancy that the voters, holding the franchise under their own State law, who freely enacted these constitutional changes and who could change them back, being a distinct political power—that notion of the old usurpation time must go with the rest to the tombs of the Capulets.

As for the fact that " these recent constitutions have decreased the dignity and influence of the commonwealth judiciary," it is all matter of daily newspaper comment, and so we can leave it ; only remembering this hint, that, if the sphere of the State judiciaries has lost less by State-constitutional limitation than the other branches, " this is again evidence of the principle that the sphere of the commonwealth government is administration rather than legislation, and judicial administration more than executive administration."*

Such being the facts, we are taught to draw an inference, founded indeed on the theory that a State of the Union always was what it was only as its administrative government was what it might be ; there being, as we have

---

* P. S. Q., I., p. 32.

been shown, no such thing, really, as a political people of a State, but only a portion of
that population which we call " the Nation."
We are told :—

" It cannot be doubted that we have in all
this a great decline in the dignity, influence,
and power of the commonwealth legislatures,
and therefore [*therefore ?*] of the commonwealths themselves. It is unmistakable that a
stronger consciousness of nationality, a larger
confidence in the national government and a
pronounced distrust of the commonwealth
governments have taken possession of the
whole people, and are now realizing themselves in the constitutional and legal transfor-
mations of our entire political system."*

The writer in our *Quarterly*, in the same
article, also says—

" The commonwealth is purely a creation of
law and is identical with its political organization. I am endeavoring, by this analysis, to
lead up the mind of the reader to the proposition that when the people resident within the
commonwealth withdraw powers from the

---

* P. S. Q., I., p. 30.

government of the commonwealth, the result is practically a change in the position of the commonwealth and not simply a redistribution of powers between different organs of the commonwealth."*

As the State or commonwealth is now to be held to exist only as its local government may subsist, it may not be very clear where the powers thus abstracted from State governments, singly, from time to time, by the people of a State, or piece of the Nation, are to go. In the times of our ignorance, " confidence in the national government " was shown only when three-fourths of the States united in placing power in its hands; while simultaneously withdrawing it from each and every State. If the doctrine of conservation of force applies in political as in physical science, the powers now withheld from the organs of States, by their recent state constitutions, ought to be somewhere ; lying round loose, perhaps, in our revolutionary era, to be picked up by the Central Government, in the sweet bye-and-bye. But though the people, so called, of a

---

* P. S. Q., I., pp. 25, 26.

State, so called, has been maiming itself while maiming its local government, the same people, so called, may, at the same time be obliged to recognize the *Commune*, wherever that may be discernible, as the only other always possible depositary for the time being: since, by the axioms of our political science, it, beside the Nation, is the only natural political reality. So we are told to observe that:—

"These more recent instruments [State constitutions] contain provisions constitutionalizing the municipal divisions of the commonwealth, *i.e.*, defending them in greater or less degree, against the power of the government of the commonwealth, securing their boundaries, establishing their organizations, defining their powers, prescribing the tenure and duties of their officers, *etc.* This is a most serious question. It demonstrates the fact that the government of the commonwealth has ceased to be in many respects the *natural* local government. It threatens the dissolution of the commonwealth through the consolidation of the municipalities." (*Note* "Counties and Cities").*

* P. S. Q., I., p 32.

Our teachers would have us observe :—

" That while the legislative and judicial powers exercised at the beginning of the century by the governments of the commonwealths are gravitating towards the national government in greater or less degree, the police powers, on the other hand, are passing over to the municipalities, and that this result is being produced as much by dissolution from within as by centralization from without, if not more."*

So we see that while the former States have been surely, though quietly, approximating to the political status of a French *Département* under a central head—King, Emperor, or Assembly—there is a local absolutism, in the hands of irresponsible majorities, gradually forming, which may find its exemplar in those peasant communities (*the Mir*) in Russia, described in Tolstoi's novels ; which have constituded the political liberty of Tartar races whenever their nomad state was merged in a territorial settlement.

When we think of New York or Chicago as

---

* P. S. Q., I., p. 33.

commune, under the irresponsible management of something like a board of Aldermen, we recall old Marshal Blücher's admiring suggestion, when, after Waterloo, his English friends showed him around London—"*Mein Gott! was für Plündern!* What a city for to sack!" Truly, "This is a most serious question"—for somebody.

We begin to learn from all this how our Revolution, started in 1787, has been a-going it. Those who all along had been regarded as governing their State, independently, as a distinct political people, by a subordinate instrumentality—legislative, executive, judicial—have, as a portion of the sovereign-Nation-people in their commonwealth, really, if perhaps unconsciously, or by a blind instinct of nationality, been revolting, piece-meal-wise, against their former selves, while apparently exercising their old political power as State, in proclaiming their several constitutions. This is just what might be expected in a continuing revolution, begun without any State's knowledge, when they ratified themselves into incipient nonentity, to be revealed in course of a century as scientific nationality.

Nobody need get disgruntled over this apparent confusion, for we can find the great balance-wheel for our constant Revolution prepared for us a hundred years agone and fully set a-going, improved and readjusted to its office in the Reconstruction time, 1865-7. As citizenship is, or is to be national, all the rights and duties of a citizen are dependent on the measure of justice given by the organ which stands for the Nation. A new meaning is to be given to, or a truer understanding has been had of the guaranty of a " republican form of government " to "every State in this Union," declared in Article IV.

It used to be supposed that it was a pledge, given by somebody, to each *State*, or political *people* of each State *in the Union*, that it should constitute an independent, self-governing body *in the Union*. But when we once understand that this *State* and this *people* of a State have no real existence, that they are like legal fictions for lawyers' use, we comprehend that the beneficiaries of the guaranty are the several portions of the Nation in geographical districts, entitled to such an administration of law for rights and duties, civil and political, as may be called *republicanism*, which should be as attainable in one commonwealth as in another.

In view of this our venerable College shows us how to modify our ancient reading of the letter which killeth, by saying :—*

" The requirement (art. 4. sec. 4) of the present constitution that the " United States " shall preserve republicanism (*sic*) in the State governments, vests in Congress the power to determine in what republican forms and institutions consist, *i.e.*, to prescribe the only legitimate form of local government which the Nation suffers to exist. . . . . The Congress has exercised the power in every enabling Act, and in the reconstruction Acts of 1867."

So that, plainly, the " United States " will execute this guaranty, not occasionally, or according to isolated exigencies of political tranquillity, as was done, it was supposed, in the case of Rhode Island, but by means of a general statute, will define *republicanism* as an individual right, comprehending life, liberty, and the pursuit of happiness, and provide for a

---

* P. S. Q. I., p. 22, *note*.

due process of law by which it may be defended in the National Courts.

Well, to know all this is to know much worth knowing; or rather, since it is presented by way of inducing scepticism, it should be to doubt much that is worth doubting. But seeing, as we do, that faith is the thing we want just at present for our jubilee and centennial, we are bound to get at it straight-off, somehow; by scientific principles and reasoning on the nature of things in general, if that may be done, or else by the bald assertion of something for the existence of which, as fact, not a shadow of evidence is produced and which is contradicted by the records that have never been disputed.

Perhaps those who have thus compelled our recognition of the continuing Revolution might have been less candid if they had been invited to celebrate with us on that last 17th of September. It should seem a singular way for us to do it by telling the world how completely the appearance of the thing born one hundred years before had belied its reality. But we have got to face the music in our own day; even though all those who preceded us should have lived in a dream. Let those doubt who may like it. We shall leave our learned teachers and those who may be content with doubting, after their fashion, to bite their nails over this sceptical or negative side of this great subject, while we attend to the affirmative ; accepting from them, as the historical basis of faith and hope, the legend, now well grown, of the Nation's Revolution in our once revered Adoption, proclaiming what we believe our supreme Government to be, in respect to us, and what we are in respect to our supreme Government.

What then is the first duty of any sovereign government? Is it not laid down or assumed by publicists, as a fundamental axiom, that the first duty of such a government is to itself ; the obligation to defend its own existence ? And is not such obligation also its right ? a right correlative to duty on the part of others ? others whose duty is submission—its own *subjects ?* Is it not the right of dominion, recognized by the world without, because exercised over the world within ?

This right or self-directed duty is paramount. To suppose that there is some law,

9

whether called a constitution or not, to restrain it is to contradict the assumption that it is a sovereign government ; for such a law presupposes a law-giver distinct from and independent of such government.

When the existence of this isolated primary right is once established, all those inconsistencies or malformations which we are now taught to regard as relics of the usurpation period—usurpation of what used to be called " State Sovereignty "—become of minor importance. For, whatever support they may have claimed from blind precedent, they will now, with our new insight, be always construed as only secondary, or even ancillary, in relation to this primary or paramount right. The States will then appear as subjects *under* law, while the Nation—in its only come-at-able representative the Central Government—is *above* law. This being understood, the written constitution may, at times, be disregarded for the preservation of this government ; as was declared by many patriotic statesmen it could, should, and was, in the civil war and in reconstruction, though there is no need of putting it so rough. Another teacher, a Professor also in another

University, who has also recently presented this discovery of the Revolutionary adoption says* —" Moreover, this boundary between federal and state powers should not be unchanging. As the conditions of national life change, it becomes necessary that the federal government should assume jurisdiction over subjects which in simpler conditions are left to the states. With a written constitution, which cannot be easily amended, it is inevitable that this transference of power should be made by interpretation. But by whatever process the change is wrought, whether by interpretation or constitutional amendment, the competence of the State is narrowed even against its will by the action of the federal state."

This was plain enough in Reconstruction, when the competency of eleven States, *if States they were*, in ratifying amendments was narrowed against their wills.

We have learned from our own College

---

* Professor Richard Hudson, University of Michigan : in the *New Englander* and *Yale Review.* January, 1888. Art. State Autonomy *vs* State Sovereignty, p. 42.

friends that " the People is a national conception and preserves its integrity against government only as a Nation." They say further :—

" Blot out the national government and you
still have the Nation physically and ethnically,
which, by its own innate power, will restore
its political organization ; but blot out the
government of the commonwealth and you
have a territory measured by the chain of the
surveyor, with a population governed exclusively by the Nation's organs and restored to
local self-government only by the Nation's
act." *

We might ask—Who is the somebody who
can do the *blotting out* in these cases? Charles
Sumner's *State-suicide* theory implied that
eleven States had blotted themselves out, as
political fact. Our professors give this statement of theirs as an old doctrine of constitutional law by adding :—

" This is really, though probably not consciously, what every judge means when he
says 'To the Government of the United
States that which has not been granted is

---

* S. P. Q., I., p. 25.

denied; but to the government of the states that which has not been denied is granted.' "

When we recall how constantly this proposition has been repeated by the highest officials, from the day when the government was first inaugurated, we see in what a topsy-turvy revolutionary chaos the whole thing has been ; so much so that the best trained minds have been misunderstanding themselves and misconstructing their own words for a whole century.

It is by understanding the true position of this sovereign Government that we shall begin to understand how, in the continued revolution, we as a people have had our political existence changed for us ; if we assume that the 14th and 15th Amendments mean something, or that "national citizenship" has come into being as never before. What sort of citizens were we before? Are we now individually, in the eyes of foreign powers anything more or less than before? If they had before recognized us, when within their jurisdictions, as *citizens* only as being the subjects of some other recognized sovereignty, has our citizenship changed in their eyes by some change in their recognition of the sovereignty; as might occur in the case of a conquest? If not, then, if our citizenship has changed at all, it must have been by change of some internal relation, not noticed by foreign powers.

If citizenship is to mean some conscious possession of political power, as legal right, has that possession been expanded or has it been limited? Does a national citizenship, in this sense, exist at all, and what is it, anyhow? What is any man's political liberty now, as an individual right?

Understanding *citizen* as one of a number of voters known as constituting a political unit, determining its own existence by discriminating the possession of the franchise, as a legal right—*citizenship* indicates a conscious possession of political right, or power—dependent only on the unit's voluntary continuance in union with other such units. While the national Government had, as adm'nistrative organ, a recognized come-at-able superior in the political people, existing as States voluntarily united, there was a *national citizenship* as a political capacity distinct from national civil citizenship or mere subjection.

But, the Central Government being regarded as a sovereign Government in its own
right, with no recognized superior but a geographical ethnical nation, as discernible by
professors of political science and the nature
of things, there is no national citizenship as a
political capacity. There are no citizens of
the nation, except as there are subjects of the
Central or Imperial Government.

No man here had been *subject* of some *one*
State. The inhabitant was always the *subject* of States—being in union, thirteen first,
more afterwards; a political fact known to the
world. Because sovereignty, the opposite of
subjection, was held by States only *as union.*
Subjection always has been national. If there
has been a change, subjection is now claimable
only by the President, Congress, and Judiciary
for the time being.

The only possible continuation for citizenship, as right not dependent on the Central
Government, was by the continued existence
of some States, not dependent on that Government, but on their own mutual recognition
as continuing in the voluntary political union.
Citizenship, under this condition, was derived

from a definite sovereign, distinct from all agents of government. When State existence and citizenship in the State may depend on the Central Government, national citizenship, as legal right, would not depend on the will of any people or Nation; or, only as there is always a possibility of revolution, by the force of a majority or minority.

Thus we ourselves continue the century of a revolution, by affirming, openly now, that sovereignty of the Nation and revolution are identical. This was Tom Jefferson's doctrine; as it has been French practice since the revolution which he witnessed.

But this Government, you may say, is, after all, only an elective government. As it is periodically renewable and renewed by election, it cannot be called a personal government. It would be impossible for those in office, at any time, to continue themselves as officers of government by continuing to use the powers exercised before; or to govern, as a monarchy or an oligarchy does, by simple continuation in a preconceived line of succession. How can this Government, while its *personnel* is elected, continue itself as against the States

or against anybody else ; as monarchs or oligarchs may have done as against the mass of
the nation ; even if it should have that control
over the electoral bodies which has been in-
dicated by sceptical criticism as essential in
the prospective development of the revolutionary adoption ?

Well then, how do monarchs and oligarchs
manage to do it ? No one thinks of the most
absolute potentate as possessing, literally,
that is in his own brawn and muscle, the
power which he directs ; seemingly of his own
will. A single human being, a Cæsar or a
Charlemagne, a Bourbon, or a Bonaparte, holds
sway only because some indefinite number of
persons, a minority, usually, in proportion to
all under his rule, believe that his possession
of political power is, more or less certainly,
for their own personal benefit. There is a
continuing collection of partisans of some sort
which makes the possibility of any absolute
ruler.

The same holds for elective governments.
While their *personnel* must experience change
by periodical dissolution and reintegration, a
distinct body of electors will continue by natu-

ral substitution. The theory of all elective systems involves personal preferences of some sort, for candidates, aside from party divisions. But all political history indicates *Parties* as inevitable under all forms of popular government. No one sees parties distinguished solely by personal preferences or mere favor or disfavor for measures, as expedient or otherwise. We see in all trans-Atlantic states parties antagonized by different faiths as to the location of that supreme power which all profess to recognize when this location is ascertained, and it is easy to conceive how, in republics, a party may arise which claims the possession of power as its right; a right which it is its first duty to defend.

The generations which have preceded our own in the century past were nursed in the belief that the republics of the future would never know a party rivalship based on such a claim; and this was because they supposed that, here, a paper constitution would hold the place of crown and sceptre—in the name of a sovereign people. Whether anything has happened since J. Q. Adams' Jubilee oration to make this questionable, or has not, we can see by the broader glare of our hundred-year-old revolution that, here, a party must take the place of that class of persons, which, in so-called autocratic countries, sustains the monarch or oligarchy, and that it will itself become our sovereign and master.

If among all parties there is one only which affirms the sovereignty of the Central Government—as founded on our legend of the century-old revolution-Government, born in the adoption of the constitution in 1787—that is the party which should alone subsist, which alone can claim *allegiance.* As such it may continue, like a dynasty, and, as such, its duty to itself and its right against others is to maintain itself for the support of that Government as sovereign.

While the revolution of 1787 was unrecognized, the States seemed continuing organizations; entities visibly holding, in union only and not severally, *all* sovereign powers; that is, both those exercised by their central organ and those exercised by their several organs of local government. When they may have been confined to administrative or police functions merely, under the Central Government, or have become geographical groups of *communes*, under a national statute guaranteeing "republicanism," according to the French ideal of political liberty in the despotism of a sovereign people, it will be inevitable that the party controlling that Central Government will have become the actual sovereign.

We may say: Parties have always existed here. It is necessary to the elective system that administration should be in the hands of the strongest party and yet no party here has had exclusive possession of administration. True ; and it is to be remembered that hith, erto, this power could not be entirely in the hands of one organ, or of a number of organs acting subordinately to some one central superior. But this has been owing entirely to the prolonged existence of those " relics of usurpation "—the States—lingering stumbling-blocks in the path of the Revolution begun by *adoption*. It is to be supposed that the party having the preponderance in the Central Government would also be the stronger in the States having the larger part of the population. But, hitherto, no one of the several parties which have existed has, at any time,

had majority-control of the Central and also
of every State Government; and, for this
reason, the entire exclusion of minorities from
the *personnel* of the Central Government has
been impossible.

When the faith, which is to follow aroused
"scepticism in politics," shall have had its
perfect work and a party shall be found whose
first principle is that the Central Government
has, at last, in our continuing Revolution,
become the only representative of sovereignty,
it will be inevitable that such party should
claim the right to determine the *personnel*
of that Government against all and every
other whose belief may conflict with its own
political faith. Its duty towards such government will be its right to maintain itself
in possession as against such others; a right
to maintain the government as its own instrument or organ; without regard to its being in
minority or majority; because all who may
not equally attribute sovereignty to that government will be in the position, essentially, of
rebels and traitors. Even if some such other
party should, by numbers and the vulgar pre-
possession for constitutional formalities, ac-

quire a preponderance, its occupation of the
Central Government should be regarded as
only a temporary *interregnum*—a passing reaction of the forces mingling in the revolutionary tide. It may sometimes be good
policy in such periods not to press the claim
of party legitimacy too far or too fast. There
may be cases—perhaps there was an example
when Tilden was *not* inaugurated—when visit-
ing statesmen can manœuvre to prevent a
party's lapse from power. In other cases of
close election, such ingenuity may have been
equally desirable, but not so prudently at-
tempted.

But we shall not falter in our faith in this
Revolution and its onward movements. We
have learned from our College what is the
approaching fate of those "three things"
which stand in the way of "complete relegation" of the States to their subordinate position in respect to "the Nation's organs of
central government."

"They are all relics of the usurpation of
1781. Whatever show of reason existed for
any of them has largely passed away, and is
now on the point of totally disappearing ; and

when the people come clearly to see that this intermeddling with the politics of the Nation is what prevents the commonwealths from properly discharging their proper functions in jural and police administration, the spirit will hardly be lacking to proceed to the transformation. For ten years now we have been passing through a period of reaction against the pronounced nationalism of the previous fifteen; but we shall come to the end of it, and the precedents are not wanting in our history to point the way for the still further nationalization of our political institutions." *

We listened a while ago, to the suggestion from a prominent weekly as to the recognition which constitutional changes in 1865-7 should have received at our centennial celebration last September. This suggestion seemed to show a glimmering appreciation of our revolutionary progression. Yet this same serene hebdomadal has remarked, *à propos* of some recent decisions of the Supreme Court.—

"It was ignorantly taken for granted that a Republican Supreme Court had all these

* P. S. Q., I., 24, 25

years been interpreting the Constitution in a way that favored the latitudinarian views of those politicians who for partisan ends have sought to aggrandize the powers of the Federal Government."*

Well, it would not be very strange if some of us should lean to latitudinarianism after a century of Revolution. "Partisan ends!" Shall colleges and professors of political science and irresistible idea be shunted off with the lobby and rings and hunters of boodle in the communes? "Ignorantly taken for granted"—Is this recognition for historical discovery and ethnical prognostication?

The editorial proceeds to proof by calling up Mr. Justice Miller as having—

"In his notable address upon the Supreme Court before the alumni of Michigan University, last summer, summed up the case, when he said: 'It may be considered now as settled that, with the exception of these specific provisions in them [the Amendments] for the protection of the personal rights of the citizens and people of the United States, and the

---

* *The Nation ;* Dec. 8, 1887, article, State Rights.

necessary restrictions upon the powers of the States for that purpose, with the additions to the power of the General Government to enforce those provisions, no substantial change has been made. The necessity of the great powers conceded by the constitution originally to the Federal Government and the equal necessity of the autonomy of the States and their power to regulate their domestic affairs remain as the great features of our complex form of government.'"

Just so. The Supreme Court says that it considers just this sort of thing quite proper, just at present, or quite necessary. But suppose the court feels differently, some day. There is no recognition here of the States as having an iota of power by right above law ; and the whole question is of that sort of right ; which is one that no court of law can determine.

" Complex form of government "—so it may seem to those who cannot accommodate their consciences to the revolution legend—the revolution of centennial adoption. Their opinions on the matter of our political obligations are far more obfuscated than were those of the foreigners who charged the Northern States with being false to their own axioms, in not acquiescing in Southern Secession. They, the foreigners, could see that a genesis by legality for a political constitution is not possible. Force, revolutionary or otherwise, must be found to support it. Our own *Quarterly* says * in another article by the same writer :—

" It seems to me, then, that an exact political science would lead us to abandon any attempt to find a *legal* justification for the manner in which the constitution of 1787 was established. We should accept fairly and fully the proposition that the constitution of 1787 rested originally upon a revolutionary basis, and justify the fact upon the principle of public necessity."

And that is as near the true statement as any one can give it : except that revolutions are a class of facts that require no justification-certificate from anybody, or from any science or system of any kind. When a man begins to talk of a revolution's having been necessary, good, desirable, or " such as political science

* P. S. Q., I., p. 619, article on Von Holst's " Public Law."

would indicate "* as establishing that there
was or was not a revolution, he stultifies
himself by assuming to judge of the existence of that which he has already asserted
as existing. The same sort of thing is done
in saying that the thirteen States, were individually sovereign before 1787—*by usurpation.*

A revolution is *a fact* by its nature ; as distinct from legislation. But both are consequences of some human will. To say, in
affirming a political change following civil
war, that "war legislates," marks the vaporous
idealist. Fact, not doctrine, nor idea, is the
foundation of all political existence. So, if
before the adoption the thirteen States were
thirteen separately sovereign nations, it was so
by virtue of the fact that so it was. Or, if
thirteen States or less than thirteen did, at
the time of this adoption, or if more than thirteen did, during the civil war, possess, together, and not severally, the powers of an
independent nation, such was the fact—without constitution for it, or law for it, or contract
under law for it, or reason for it, or political

† P. S. Q., I., p. 620.

science for it, or consent of anybody but themselves, *as States* existing in political union, for it.   But lawyers and judges, as is their nature, will fancy, with Mr. Justice Miller, that they can find law for the existence of the law-giver.

Revolutions have been likened to volcanic eruptions.   On Vesuvius they have what they call an observatory : not to watch stars, but the volcano : to note the glowing crater, the rumblings, the brimstone vapor and, above all, the shakings of the mountain.   For this they have what they call a seismograph—earthquake-recorder.   Our Supreme Court at the Capitol, seated between the Senate Chamber and Hall of Representatives, may be like a seismograph between two craters of a volcano always more or less eruptive.   It can record the earthquake and perhaps give warning of the lava-flow.   If it will be part of a revolutionary sovereign government, it must be more than a court of *law* in the true sense of that word, and may learn in time that there is no *law* to give or withhold sovereignty.

What does Senator Hawley know about *adoption* when he assumes to say that "the tendency towards consolidation of the entire

powers of the government is one of the strongest to-day and one of those most dangerous to
the republican experiment as our fathers understood it?" The fact being, however, that
we, a hundred years later, understand our fathers' understanding a great deal better than
they understood it themselves.

We who know that our citizenship has become subjection, and who know it because we
know where to find our sovereign, are clear on
this point of our obligations. We who recognize the revolutionary basis of the supreme
Central Government shall of necessity present
ourselves, collectively, as the Legitimist Party,
to which, individually, we shall give our allegiance, independently of men or measures. If
any ask how our party can be recognized and
distinguished from others, when perhaps we
may not, as a party, have complete control of
all government, central as well as local, we
shall claim identification, historically, with
those whose fortune it was to have principally
directed the Government during the civil war
and the Reconstruction era : assuming, from
the arguments of the leaders, at that time,
that they did this on the principle of devotion

to a supreme or sovereign government, then recognized by them as superior to all States North or South, united or disunited, and therein making the position of that government, during the war, intelligible and politically consistent :—intelligible and consistent in itself, but especially as compared with its position under any other explanation of our political institutions which had ever been set up by any other party proposing to support the government in that crisis, while still adhering to the historical doctrine, or assumption, of an originally separate sovereignty in the several States.

This party it is which, from its record in that crisis and with the new discovery of its basis in old revolution, can claim the titles of The Great and Historical Party, as compared with others, old or new, and which now takes its stand as Legitimist, by the right of the Central Government to claim personal allegiance, as being a personal government, now seen to have rested one hundred years—not on social compact, federal compact or any such fiction of fetish-constitution-mongers, but on fact, historical fact—the Revolution in the

adoption of the written Constitution of 1787.
Here then, at last, Americans can find a
party with a principle which is perennial—a
principle which can be distinguished from following men or pursuing measures; a principle which is *loyalty*—not to a form of words, a
statute, a paper constitution, nor to a form of
government—but loyalty to persons, that is,
to the party itself. For we see that, in order
to recognize in the Central Government a personal sovereign, and to support it as such, the
party must affirm its own personal right to
create that government. In the nature of
such a party this loyalty is its only *principle*,
in the true sense of the word. To this, measures are means, not ends. By this, men's
qualifications and characters as candidates for
office are to be estimated; or rather, we
should say, their qualifications and characters
need not be estimated at all. To be the candidate of the party is character and qualifica-
tion.

So, in behalf of such a party, it could well
be said by an orator :—" The general judgment
of the American people is that you must vote
for your principles, and for those who agree

with you in principle"; and by an organ of its
policy:—"Any citizen, even the most intelligent, may be deceived in regard to the character of a candidate. Just as the shrewdest
business men are constantly suffering from
misplaced confidence in adroit scamps, so that
the plausible demagogue finds a new crop of
deluded victims every season. But the plain
citizen need never be deceived if he inquire
honestly regarding the beliefs and tendencies
of a great historical party. He can know
with absolute certainty in what directions its
power will be exerted."

And right you are, this time, dear old *Tri-
bune !* While the beautifulest of it all is that
other contestants for power fancy that they
can get on without any such faith in themselves as sovereign—that is, without claiming
loyalty for themselves, as party having a divine right to rule—because they have never
been able to find a personal sovereign anywhere.

Such other possible parties are obliged to
profess that the only issues in practical politics
are as to measures of administration ; or, that
such measures are to be judged by considera-

tions of utility and legal constitutionality; without reference to knowledge of any intrinsic relation of superiority and inferiority held by the Central Government and the States reciprocally. So it has always been with them. And, therefore, these other parties never could give an explanation, when they affirmed the duty of the citizen to support the Central Government in a crisis like that of 1861–5; that is, none comparable for logical consistency with that which we now base on the discovery of actual revolution in the adoption of 1787; whereby that sovereignty came to an end, which all parties used to assume had belonged to each State of the thirteen, in severalty.

From their failure to recognize this revolution, these other parties have been forced, at all times since the adoption, to appear as supporters of that doctrine of State-sovereignty which all the outside world regarded as proving that the adoption was no more than an act of confederation between sovereigns; and as justifying the claims of the Southern Confederacy to international recognition on their secession; and which would of itself have secured that recognition, if there had been no question of moral sympathy or repugnance with slavery; and which, as it is, has made the Northern charge of treason on the part of the Confederacy, or its citizens, seem to all the world an absurdity.

In this imbecility of every other party lies the present strength of our grand old party of historic legitimacy, begun in Revolution. For even when not holding such thorough control of the Central Government as it had from 1860 to a recent period, the party can secure support from the forces of its purblind adversaries for measures which it would naturally promote in supporting its own views of centralization, and which, therefore, must facilitate its own return to power, and secure its possession in the future.

The dullest can see that, as precedent to be used in some later affirmation of our own Legitimist position, when the time comes, it is as useful, or even better, that another party, having temporary preponderance in the Central Government, should, for its own partisan ends, have interfered in State elections and blindly deserted its own traditions. Be-

sides, as long as any other parties, not accepting our legitimist doctrine, are possible, it will
be politically expedient for us to endure the
customary survival of those "relics of usurpation"—the States ; being careful, however, to
ignore any pretension to their individual or
collective possession of original power and to
avoid any language warranting an inference
that they had held *reserved* powers, or that the
powers which have been or may be exercised
by the Central Government had ever been
granted or *delegated* to it as agent, instead of
having been assumed, among the whole sum
of sovereign powers, by right above law, because founded on Revolution.   Thus, once on
a time, in years before its days of grandeur,
our great historical party in convention in 1860,
could say—

"*Resolved*, That the maintenance inviolate
of the rights of the States, and especially the
right of each State to order and control its
own domestic institutions according to its own
judgment, exclusively, is essential to that balance of power on which the perfection and endurance of our political fabric depends."

What was there in this to limit future

action ? This being, at the most, the party's approval of whatever it might at any time deem " essential " to the perfection and endurance of our political fabric. There was here no recognition of political rights in the sense of political powers. When the day of party-power came, the essence of our political fabric was found to lie all in the existence of a Central Government, alone representing the sum and substance of all independent political dominion.

All this goody-goody talk can be repeated at any time. It is much like the Supreme Court's informing* us that "under the pressure of all the excited feeling growing out of the war, our statesmen have still believed that the existence of the States with powers for domestic and local government . . . . was essential to the perfect working of our complex form of government, though they [*our statesmen*—mind you !] have thought proper to impose additional limitations upon the States, and to confer additional powers on that of the

---

* Quoted in Mr. Justice Miller's Michigan University Address from the opinion in the Slaughter-House Cases.

United States. But whatever fluctuations may be seen in the history of public opinion on this subject, during the period of our national existence, we think it will be found that this court, so far as its functions required, has always held with a steady and an even hand the balance between State and Federal power, and we trust that such may continue to be the history of its relation to that subject so long as it shall have duties to perform which demand of it a construction of the constitution, or of any of its parts."

If the court, or "our statesmen," or anybody else, has engaged to consider always the best interests of the States and allow them as much self-government as is for the good of people in general—everybody is greatly obliged to them for their benevolent designs. But when we once have comprehended that this *subjection* of ours rests on a Revolution begun a century ago by "the natural leaders of the Nation," though hardly yet perfected, even by "the men of 1861–7," or "our statesmen," as the court puts it, who improved on the work of the men of 1787, we know where we are and can accept the situation.

With this conception of loyalty we may always promote any single measures, by whomsoever proposed, which make our States or "commonwealths" recipients of the Central Government's indulgence or assistance : just as provinces, cities or communes are proper subjects of favorable or unfavorable attentions under more fully centralized sovereignties. Surplus revenue can be distributed here and there, like candy to children at Christmas— to keep them or make them good. Works of internal improvement will suggest themselves, as convenient in making just discrimination among localities ; or bounties to make the industries of some districts appear profitable.

And in this connection, we shall all see the extreme propriety in providing the Government with an overflowing treasury ; far above the insignificant savings from an income which the revolutionary adopters of a century ago imagined sufficient for a government " to provide for the common defence, promote the general welfare and secure the blessings of liberty." In fact, a continuing war-revenue-standard should be enthusiastically advocated ; in view of the fact that our Legitimist party has always boasted that, with its support, the Central Government had, as sovereign, maintained itself by war ; and we may naturally expect to use methods equally costly in dollars, if not in lives, to sustain its existence in the future.

It is clear too that it will be conducive to the same ends to favor, *incidentally*, the activities of persons who, being *directly* enriched by receiving, as a class, *protection* through the operation of an *indirectly* raised revenue, will continue to look for it to the Central Government ; and who, having benefited by this means at the expense of other subjects of that Government, may be expected to aid in sustaining by their wealth the Legitimist principle of loyalty, since such protection could never be afforded by any of the local governments ; however willing they might be, to say nothing of those States whose resources might be impaired by such methods of promoting the general welfare.

Similar considerations will indicate that for some time to come a passive policy, in some directions, may also be advantageous, whether our actual party-preponderance be

immediate or only prospective. Some political experiments which would appear eminently
proper in view of identifying the Central Government with the entire People, as sovereign,
may well be kept in abeyance. For example,
the anomaly in the existence of five adjoining
States in the eastern portion, together not
equal in territory to one of several others,
with their disproportionate representation in
the Senate, may remain unnoticed, as long as
the industries of their inhabitants would
marshal them among the supporters of our
party of Legitimacy and swell majorities to
sustain the financial methods it advocates.

Besides, are we not in honor bound to respect localities whose intellectual activity has
so manipulated the biographies of our forefathers as to disclose the historical foundation
of our sovereign Central Government? It is
mainly due to the literary activity of our *Doctrinaires*, in this little group of States and in
their Western affiliations, that we, as a party,
have learned how to assert our Legitimist
position—sovereign by the Grace of God, by
the necessity of things, by Revolution. Who
else can pretend to retain a disproportion of

political power in State existence, if not those who, by heredity, can claim that their conception of right and wrong must be received as *law* by every one else?

In such recognition of intellectual pre-eminence in a small portion of our wide dominion, we may also show our appreciation of all the men of learning who are now crowding along from East and West to aid our College in upholding the dynastic idea founded on the discovered Revolution. All ordinary party strategy is indeed nothing comparable to our making friends with the literary fellows—*genus irritabile* though they be.

It has been the folly and weakness of other parties that they have taken small account of "culture" and never understood what a few despised scribblers have often done in shaping the world's destiny. Their simple state-craft mocks at nationalism—cooked up by study of physical geography and ethnical affinities, and at discrimination of sovereign peoples by linguistic traditions beginning with the tower of Babel. As to history, they are ready enough to say—"Let the dead past bury its dead," but never seeing that there is no reality in the

things of the present except as they continue
the things of the past.　The best they can do,
in the way of political dogma, is to repeat
with the Supreme Court the meaningless
apothegm—"an indestructible union of indestructible and immutable States"—to their
own confusion.

Let them ridicule our Professors for emulat-
ing French *Doctrinaires*, like Lamartine, in
political sentimentalism, and for preaching the
positive philosophy of Auguste Comte, as re-
ligion and law in one, and proclaiming at once
the war of ideas and the gospel of humanity.
Not having any such school of the prophets
to mould and polish their political vagaries
into a presentable form, their managers are
obliged to put their trust in slang-wanging
editorials, caucus, bar-room politicians, tough
boys, ballot-stuffings, jobs for the boodle and
in "tricks that are vain."

To those who know how the world is moved
by thought, *Education* is a word of power.
To us, who propose that the thought which
is to move others shall be of our own thinking,
Education is as a talisman in the hand of the
adept.　It is the boast of modern Prussia that

the school-master has done more than the re-
cruiting sergeant of great Fritz's time towards
giving her the hegemony of Germany. All
the older dynasties have learned that, with
education in their hands, they can well afford
to profess subjection to public opinion.

Education! And what is Civil Service Re-
form, when regarded in relation to such a
party as ours, but a branch of *education?* For
this service a Central Government requires
educated men. Education is a grand thing;
for is it not a grand thing to be educated?
Educated, above all, in knowing who it is one
must obey, in the last resort, as sovereign.
The country needs above all, men who know
and can show this, and this can only be known
and shown by education—education in *loyalty*.
We are under deep obligations to isolated professors in so many colleges and universities for
these discoveries in our history which lay a
solid foundation for our supremacy. These
discoveries should be secured by means of one
grand national instrument of education. We
should profit by the examples of France and
Germany; and have every school in the land
subordinated to a central university, main-

tained from the superabundant means given by an overflowing treasury in our hands. And why should not we too have things orna- mental, but also useful as exciting literary em- ulation, like the Royal Society—F.R.S. gentle- men ; Members of the *Institût*, of the *Academie Française*, etc., to gather about us a body of decorated supporters of our Central Govern- ment ?

Indeed what a grand thing it would be to have a government carried on throughout by literary men—of the right sort, of course ! Did not Lowell—one of our best known liter- ary men—only the other day, quote before us, Bacon, as "a man versed both in affairs and books," for saying : "and, for the matter of policy and government ; that learning should rather hurt than enable thereunto is a thing very improbable ; " and, " It cannot but be a matter of doubtful consequence if states be managed by empiric statesmen, not well min- gled with men grounded in learning. But, contrariwise, it, is, almost without instance contradictory, that ever any Government was disastrous that was in the hands of learned governors." And it has been quite common of late years, in England and France, particularly, to see eminence in literature regarded as recommendation either for suffrages of the voters or for appointment to office. But such popular recognition of individual accomplishments is not what we should encourage as good example. Our idea of government by literary men should be to have a properly educated class created, properly sifted by civil service examinations—as to *loyalty* especially —for material for our elections or appointments. This is not by any means an experiment. We can point to one of the greatest, the oldest, the most stable of all existing empires for an illustration.

There's China—The Chinese Empire—you know. Well: there they have had dynasty after dynasty—whatever that may be; the present dynasty is number twenty and a good deal more. But, practically, they have for ages been governed by one set of men—their literary fellows. With them, civil service examinations are as old and older than the Great Wall. Examinations that last for weeks, that are no joke. The young fellows have to study Confucius and Mencius; old authors who wrote exclusively about virtue—public and private virtue—and be posted on the piles of commentators on these.　Well: if the Chinese officials are, as all travellers tell us, the most venal, unrighteous, tyrannical set of bureaucrats the world knows of?　Well:—why even Bacon, Lord of Verulam and Viscount of St. Albans, had his snarling detractors, who impeached him, as chancellor-judge, for taking bribes.　And they mocked at his learning and called him names.　For, as he said, " It hath been ordinary with politique men to extenuate and disable learned men by the name of pedants "—*doctrinaires*, Lowell says, is the word to-day.　Well, but the educated Chinese keep on having the offices and sustaining their Central Government all the same.　If education and civil service examinations will do that for those Chinese fellows, what may we not expect when our Professors of Political Science run the machine with books on public virtue all beginning with the Revolution by adoption!　If the Chinese Mandarins do the way they do do, it must be because the way they do is to do the way their ancestors did. They worship the graves of their ancestors:

annually and all the time. So that the practical application of Confucius on virtue is settled by what has always been the application. We, just about this time, are venerating the monuments of our forefathers of a hundred years ago, and we have learned something about their virtue in the business of adoption. Their example binds us to no stand-still policy. And, if they now appear not to have known much what they were about, why should we pretend to greater foresight. Revolution was their choice. We too are adopters. Revolution should be ours, progressing on high moral and intellectual ideas.

In the mean time men of any party, or of no party, may in a certain sense sustain the Central Government: in their obeying the laws and constitution, voting for good persons for Presidents and Congress, or in seeking office and influence, as under some administration, on the strength of their personal antecedents. But there is no *loyalty* in all this. Anybody is free to do this or to leave it alone. It will be only those who support the Central Government on the Legitimist basis and as claiming sovereign rights for "the great historical party," who will be truly *loyal* as men are loyal to monarchs in other lands. As private subjects, we will show our loyalty by simply voting for the candidates of this party, regardless of their personal valuation. To use the expression attributed to a Massachusetts Senator of a past generation—"a nomination, eminently unfit to be made, may be eminently fit to be supported;" and, to borrow the unctuous phrase of a Massachusetts Senator of to-day. "A man cannot serve God and Baal." When the question is of allegiance, the subject who proposes to be Independent is a traitor. Those who, while pretending to be still of us, refuse this test of fidelity are apostates as well; far more guilty of treason than those who, never having been shown the historic truth of a century-old Revolution, may be seeking to find their sovereign elsewhere, by rummaging among the records of those "relics of usurpation," the States in union.

In this way it will be that, as Garfield truly said when in Congress, ideas will be the only sovereigns; with only one more question to answer :—Whose ideas?

It must be an issue between *men* of different ideas—not better distinguishable, perhaps, than as "we 'uns" and "you 'uns," according to the expressive nemenclature of the ruder Southrons in the war. John Morley remarks that "Rousseau's whole theory tends inevitably to substitute a long series of struggles after phrases and shadows, in the new era, for the equally futile and equally bloody wars of dynastic succession which have been the great curse of the old. Men die for a phrase as they used to die for a family."

Issues between ideas—sovereign ideas—could be decided only as issues between sovereign flesh and bone are decided,—by "blood and iron."

We who in our contests for place and power every day proclaim the sovereignty of *our* ideas as proved by the ordeal of battle, will yet long display from our platforms and our pulpits the garments rolled in the blood of civil war: imitating from a distance of ages, the chariot of the crimson-robed Imperator, followed by cringing Senate and degenerated people, exulting in the spectacle of a Roman

Triumph for the subjugator of a despairing Republic.

But ideas are of no one country. As sovereign, their sovereignty is cosmopolitan. So we are more than a mere party existing in or for one country or nation only—we who support the sovereignty of our own ideas. We say with Auguste Comte, in concluding· his grand work on Positive Politics—

" In the name of the Past and the Future— the servants of Humanity—both its philosophical and its practical servants—come forward to claim as their due the general direction of this world. Their object is to constitute at length, a real Providence in all departments, moral, intellectual and physical," *etc., etc.*

" The American people are not regardful simply of their own sovereignty. They have an outlook also beyond themselves and a successful party with them, while national, must be international as well. It must have large human interests. * * * Our most conspicuous national trait is the breadth of our human sympathy. We recognize our relationship to all the world * * * We do not even claim our national privileges on the ground of our national peculiarities * * * We claim ours, not for the reason that we are Americans, but that we are men. * * * This fact makes another line of party success clear. * * * That party with us is likely to be most successful in which the unerring instinct of the people finds the largest sense of our organic unity with all mankind." So says Julius H. Seelye, President of another college.*

By rushing onward in the battle of ideas we place ourselves in solidarity with revolutionists everywhere: with those who in Europe call themselves the International—the Party of the Revolution—Revolution anywhere and everywhere. We are of them: they are of us. We are all "men without a country." Let them come along: the Communist, the Anarchist, the Socialist, or whatever else! We are all in the swim! *Vogue la galère!* Let her go, Gallagher! *Vive la Commune !!*

---

* Amherst, Mass., Article, "Our Political Prospects," in *The Forum*, March 1888, p. 5.

www.ingramcontent.com/pod-product-compliance
Lightning Source LLC
Chambersburg PA
CBHW031115020726
47495CB00007B/2211